CONFRONTING THE CHAOS

A SPECULATIVE FICTION NOVELLA

THE NEXT HIGH PRIEST
BOOK 2

PETER DEHAAN

- Developmental editor: Julie Harbison
- Copyeditor: Robyn Mulder
- Cover design: Fanderclai Design
- Author photo: Chelsie Jensen Photography

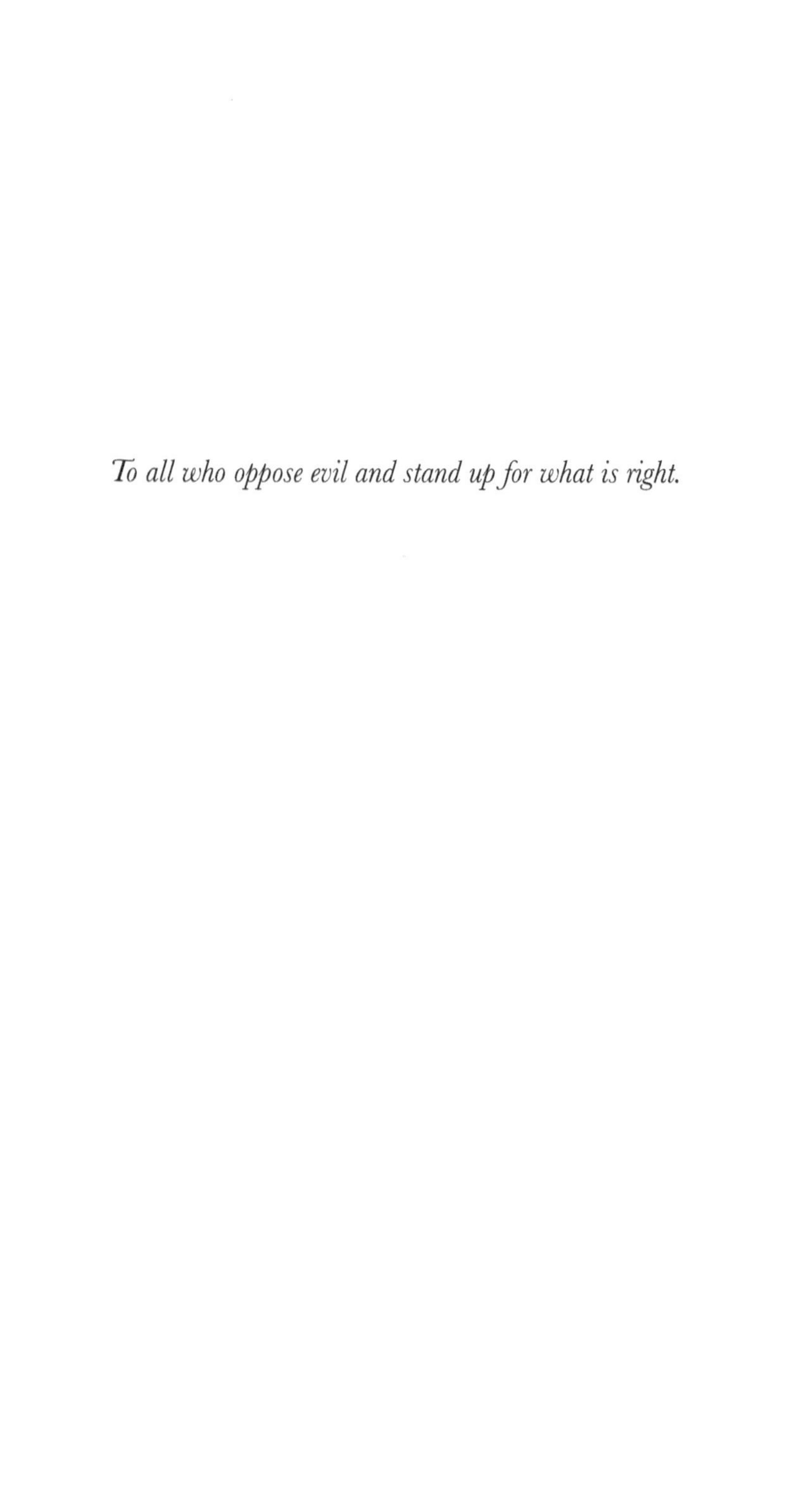

To all who oppose evil and stand up for what is right.

CONTENTS

CONFRONTING THE CHAOS

In a world just like ours . . . only different

The words of a false friend inflict wounds more deep than sword or arrow; they tear down and destroy. Whereas the words of a true friend heal, restore, and strengthen; they can even raise up priests the people will trust. -Wisdom 7.241

1
———

ALIVE

Emma shifted under the weight of warm covers. Yet something was wrong. This wasn't her bed. It didn't feel like her room. A surge of panic coursed through her body. *Where am I? What has happened?* She urged her eyes to open—and failed.

Why can't I focus? Groggy best described her mind. *Why is it so hard to move?* Or maybe achy better defined how she felt. Which was it? A confused mind or a sore body? It was too much to sort out. She couldn't concentrate. For now, she'd settle on groggy *and* achy. Her fleeting reality slipped away. Slumber overtook her.

Emma didn't know if it was seconds, minutes,

or hours later when her eyes fluttered open for a moment and then flitted shut. *Where am I?* She yawned and stretched with a groan. *Why does my entire body throb?*

"I think she's finally waking up," a voice said. It sounded familiar.

"Mom?" Emma croaked. She reached out a hand to touch the voice, but, encountering nothing, her weak arm dropped helplessly to the bed. Emma sighed. Someone stroked her hand. Warm. Comforting. Safe.

"I'm right here, dear," her mom said. "We all are. Your dad and your sister and brother. Chloe and a girl named Sarah are waiting outside."

"What happened?" Emma moaned. Something was wrong. She forced her eyes open and squinted.

The image of her mom came into focus. She sat in a chair next to the bed. "You're in the High Priest's residence in the Temple Palace. I'll explain everything later, but first we need to make sure you're all right."

"I'm fine. My mind's a bit foggy. I'm sore too. I don't think that's going away anytime soon." With care, Emma shifted in the oversized bed, one far larger than she'd ever slept in—or even seen.

A jolt of pain shot from her right calf to her left shoulder, traveling through her back. She yelped as if shocked by a surge of electricity. "Ouch!" As the pain ebbed, she let out a controlled breath.

"Where does it hurt?" Her dad rose from his chair.

Emma shifted her gaze to him. "All over."

"Describe it."

She moved her arm with care and gave an unconcerned wave with the back of her hand. She wasn't being disrespectful because she knew in her spirit she was okay—at least she *would* be. She merely needed to give it time.

Her dad opened his mouth as if to protest but then closed it, saying nothing.

"When did you last eat, Emma?" Concern coated her mom's question.

With effort, Emma shifted her attention—foggy as it was—back to her mom. "I ate breakfast this morning at Sarah's."

"You mean Thursday?" Her mom sounded confused. "Before school?"

"Yes, that's what I said. This morning."

"Emma," her mom said gently, "today is Saturday. It's after noon. You've been sleeping for over twenty-four hours."

"I guess that's why I'm so hungry. And why I so need to pee." Emma let go of her mom's hand and, with effort, eased off the blankets. Taking her time, she slid her legs to the side of the bed and willed her body upright. At least she tried to. Her head spun, and she fell back onto the bed with a grunt. She stared helplessly at the ceiling.

"Do you want us to help you?"

Emma forced her eyes to take in the whole room to see who *us* referred to. Her mom stretched out a hand. Her dad stood next to her mom. The twins kept vigil at the foot of the bed, concern painted on their uncharacteristically cherub faces. With a deliberate slowness, Emma sat up again and extended both arms. Her mom took one and her dad held the other. Leaning on them for support, she stood, but she didn't know which direction to head. "Ah, where's the bathroom?"

Her sister giggled. "We've found at least six so far. The closest one is over there." Hailey pointed to Emma's right. Her parents guided her in that direction.

When finished, she caught her reflection in the bathroom mirror. She paused in distress at what looked back at her. Having not been washed in three days, her hair showed it, no longer clean and fluffy—instead, oily and matted.

She pushed the tangled, hazel mess away from her face, which revealed a smear of dirt across her left cheek and a zit about ready to erupt on her forehead. Lacking her compact or any other helpful resources, all she could do was scrape her fingernail over it to release the pressure. It worked. Sort of. *Gross. Oh, so gross.*

She corralled her hair and—lacking a hair clip or ponytail holder—she looped it over itself in a loose knot. It would have to do for now.

She shuffled back to the bed on her own and fell into it with a moan. "Maybe after I get something to eat, I'll be strong enough to take a shower. I feel gross." She ran her tongue over her teeth. *Definitely gross.*

Her dad tipped his head toward her brother, who scurried from the room. Emma hoped he was going to round up some food.

"What's the last thing you remember?" Dad asked.

Emma's mind clawed through a jumbled heap of memories. One image emerged and became clearer. "I spent the night in the Temple and talked with the Sovereign about giving us a new High Priest."

Her parents shared concerned glances.

"I never wanted it to be me."

Her mom raised an eyebrow toward Emma's dad.

Emma clawed her mind for clarity. Some images emerged, faint at first and then clearer. "In the morning, there was a confrontation outside with the SWAT team. The captain was mad and . . . he shot at me with his machine gun." Emma gasped at the thought. "But the bullets fell to the ground before they hit me." She glanced at her chest to make sure she was okay. "The Sovereign protected me."

Emma's mind struggled to recall what happened next. "I sent the captain back to the prison to release Joshua—to free all the prisoners wrongly arrested."

Emma shut her eyes as she struggled to pull the next events from her mind. "There were a lot of people there . . . and the media with their cameras and mics. I don't know if I said something to the crowd or just thought about it . . . The next thing I remember is waking up here."

"You did, indeed, speak to the crowd," her dad

said. "The media captured everything and broadcast it across the country—around the world. You're a hero, by the way. We couldn't be prouder.

"The grand celebration lasted for hours," he added. "More and more people kept arriving. Thousands, for sure. I suspect even ten. You thanked them for coming and showing their support. Then you excused yourself to get some needed rest. You went back into the Temple and collapsed just inside."

That last part was a blur. Emma couldn't decide if she remembered that happening or merely wanted to.

"What you went through is unprecedented," her dad said. "The medical community has no explanation for what your body—and your mind—endured throughout all that happened to you. Both the night spent in the Temple—which has killed everyone else or drove them to madness—and your body repelling bullets."

"The Sovereign protected me." This was all the explanation Emma could offer—and all that she needed. "I'm sore, and it's hard to focus, but I'm okay. Or at least I will be."

"Though you underwent an extraordinary trauma, I can confirm your body hasn't suffered as a result. Your temperature is normal, your pulse is steady, and your heart is strong. As a doctor, I prescribe rest. As your father, I'm nonetheless concerned."

"I'm fine. No worries."

But am I?

2

UNTIL YOU DIE

Emma's brother paraded into the room. All eyes turned toward him.

Brayden arrived empty-handed, but four people trailed behind him. Dressed in white, each attendant carried a tray of food. They arranged the vast spread around Emma on the gigantic bed.

One tray held breakfast foods: scrambled eggs and cheese, vanilla yogurt, buttered toast and jam, bacon, and an assortment of diced melons. Another tray overflowed with meats: sliced ham, a roast smothered in gravy, and crispy fried chicken. The breads tray had buttery rolls, blueberry muffins, artisanal bread, and savory-looking tarts. Rounding out the feast was a tray of salads.

The intermingling aromas of warm bread, roast beef, and melted cheese filled Emma with anticipation. She inhaled deeply and licked her lips.

"Pull up a chair. Let's eat." Gingerly, Emma shifted upright, resting her back on the headboard. "Get Chloe and Sarah too."

Her family and friends insisted they weren't hungry. It took a bit of coaxing, but Brayden started eating. Soon all the others joined in. It was a feast, just like at their family Fall Festival observance.

Emma scarfed down the food, trying a bit of everything. It tasted so good. Energy pulsed through her body, reinvigorating her sore muscles and loosening her stiff joints. Peace flowed into her soul.

Aside from the awkwardness of being in bed with everyone else sitting around and staring at her, it was a grand celebration.

"Yes!" Sarah's shriek startled everyone. All eyes darted in her direction. She beamed at her phone and pumped her fist in the air. "Joshua's in processing and will be released soon. Gotta bounce." With that, she scooted out of the room.

"Who's Joshua?" Brayden asked.

"He's Sarah's brother," Emma answered, "and my boy . . . Joshua is my friend. He's a boy."

"Boyfriend," Chloe coughed into her hand. As a

sly smirk played at the corners of her mouth, she stood. "I need to go too. Sarah's my ride." Then she clarified. "Her parents are in the Temple praying. *They're* my ride."

Chloe left and everyone resumed eating. To Emma's relief, no one mentioned the *boyfriend* remark. But there'd be plenty of teasing later, once everyone knew she was okay.

Why did I almost say boyfriend? And why did Chloe say it? Do I actually like Joshua?

Emma shook off the notion. Using her mind, she reached into the spiritual realm. Studying her family, she looked for auras, which revealed the Divine Spirit residing within. She saw none. Though she did see colors, which she assumed was a prerequisite to receive the Divine Spirit. But that was just a guess.

Her parents had the faintest traces of indigo, while the twins gave off lilac vibes. Emma sighed, hopefully to herself. Maybe one day they could have the Divine Spirit live within them too.

As they wrapped up their meal, an official-looking man paraded in. He looked a tad familiar. He sported jet-black hair that boasted a distinguished tint of gray, slickly combed back to reveal a pale, gaunt face. He was older than her dad but younger than her spiritual mentor, Gabe.

An ornate beige robe with layered folds draped around his lanky body. The robe covered all but his pale face and hairy hands. He interlaced his fingers and kept them clasped before him. His countenance portrayed calm, looking as though nothing could ever rattle him. Yet, he had no aura and no color to his essence. Just black. A glossy black.

"Joy fills my soul knowing that you are recovering," the composed man said. "May your sustenance provide you strength for what lies ahead."

He said all this without altering his expression. Though he said the right words, Emma doubted he meant a single one.

"If you will all please excuse us, the High Priestess and I have much to discuss." His gaze scanned Emma's family gathered around the bed, communicating clearly that this was not a request but a demand. Emma's mom hugged her, the rest waved their goodbyes, and everyone filed out.

The unwanted visitor pulled a chair to the edge of the bed. Emma tried to mask her discomfort at him being so close. *Should I ask him to move away?* Yet he didn't look like a man who'd take kindly to requests, especially from a fifteen-year-old girl. *I so wish Dad hadn't left.*

"Who are you?" Emma asked, trying to sound casual and not reveal her fear.

"You may call me Your Royal Eminence," he said with an edge to his voice, as if she should know.

"Sorry. You look different than on TV . . . and older too."

The man stiffened. He glared at her.

Emma strained to suppress what she wanted to say next, but failed. "There's nothing royal about you. You don't have an ounce of royalty in you."

"Your Eminence is acceptable too."

"Do you have a name?"

"My title is Chief of Priests. You may call me Chief, if you must."

Emma curled her lip as she considered each suggestion. *You're so pompous, a pompous jack . . .* Right then she determined to call him nothing to his face and Pompous Jack to his back.

"That was quite the little stunt you pulled yesterday. You enthralled the masses, with you being so young, and a female besides." For the first time, Pompous Jack's lips twitched, the corners turning up just a bit. "I still can't ascertain how you accomplished it. Those falling bullets would have certainly been difficult to fake."

"The Sovereign is a most amazing deity." Emma wasn't sure if deity was a suitable label or one that revealed how little she knew about her emerging faith.

"Don't pretend the Sovereign had something to do with what transpired. We both know better."

"It certainly wasn't me. It had to be the Sovereign."

"Be that as it may, we must discuss your role in tomorrow's service. The people are clamoring to see you and to hear you speak. Don't worry, though, I'll do all the heavy lifting. You only need to show up and say what I tell you to."

"If it's all the same to you," Emma said with a calm firmness that surprised her, "I just want to go home and take a shower."

"You amuse me, little one. You cannot go home. That door is closed. You made certain of that when you presumed to seize the position of High Priestess." He gestured to the surrounding space with both arms. "As much as it distresses me, this is your new home. And you will live here until the day you die."

3

FITTING

"I don't want to live here." Emma set her jaw and scowled.

"You should have considered that before you inserted yourself into the role of High Priestess." Pompous Jack stood and crossed his arms, glaring down at her.

"I never asked to be High Priestess." Still in bed, Emma crossed her arms, too, and locked eyes with his. "I merely asked the Sovereign to provide one. Besides, I'm too young and I'm still in school. Plus, I'm a girl, and every High Priest has been a guy. I never wanted this to happen."

"Yet you made certain it did."

"But my friend Gabe said I wasn't the One."

"I have no clue what you're referring to.

Regardless, I've summoned the tailor to alter a robe to fit you for tomorrow's service. He'll arrive sharply at three o'clock."

"A robe?" Emma raised an eyebrow, a trait she'd inherited from her mom.

"You'll give a short welcome to start the service and conclude with a blessing. Just two simple sentences. I'll do everything else. Do you think you can handle that?"

"I'm used to being in front of people," Emma said. "I've been in several plays at school and two community theater productions. So, yes, I can handle it." She maintained her steady stare at Pompous Jack. Whoever blinked first would lose, and it wouldn't be her. "But it doesn't really matter what I think, does it?"

After an interminable time, he broke first, spun around, and stomped out the door.

While Emma waited for the tailor, she said goodbye to her family, explaining only that she planned to spend the night at the High Priest's residence in the Temple Palace. They left, and she hopped in the shower to clean her body and clear her mind.

The warm water caressed her skin and soothed the aches that lingered from yesterday's ordeal.

Although now clean and odor free, Emma's only clothes were the outfit she'd worn for the last two and a half days and nights. She now sympathized with Gabe's homelessness, realizing that even when he bathed, he had only dirty clothes to put back on. No wonder he reeked.

With fifteen minutes to spare, Emma spent the time exploring her new "home." The multi-level mansion was showy, spacious, and sprawling. Room after room, everything repelled her. She'd never been in a place like this and had only seen such a grandiose display of excessive living on television. The whole place disgusted her. She just wanted to go home.

She found the six bathrooms and then three more. She lost track of the number of bedrooms. Aside from those, there was a grand foyer, a formal dining room, four sitting rooms, and two kitchens—one large and showy and the other small and practical.

Along with multiple rooms of undiscernible purpose, she discovered two meeting spaces. The first was cozy and ideal for two or three people. The other was a large conference room with a mahogany table and an array of luxurious, black leather chairs.

Connecting them was a flashy office. Papers strewn across the desk showed recent use. Emma suspected Pompous Jack had claimed this space as his own.

He can have it because I'm getting out of here as soon as I can.

A gong reverberated through the Temple Palace. It was three o'clock, and she assumed the tailor had arrived. She made her way to the foyer to let him in, but a servant had already done so and disappeared just as stealthily.

A thin man with a solemn face, her visitor wore a smartly-tailored suit with a subtle, baby-blue-colored tie. He made a slight bow before her. "I'm honored, My Lord, to attend to your wardrobe needs." His body straightened, but his eyes carefully avoided Emma's.

He carried the most repulsive piece of clothing she'd ever seen. It was worse than she'd imagined. A passive gray. Formal. Sterile. She wrinkled her nose as its musty scent assaulted her. She didn't even think to ask his name.

"You expect me to wear that?"

"Please accept my deepest apologies, My Lord. With such short notice, we'll have to make do with this and alter it for tomorrow's ceremony. But be assured, I'll make you a robe worthy of your size and stature for next week."

Emma wasn't sure if *size and stature* was a put-down or a sign of respect, so she said nothing. She also wasn't sure where to direct the man for her fitting, but she felt the foyer was an inappropriate place, the same for the bedrooms and bathrooms.

"No one has worn this robe in decades, but it's the closest one we have to your frame. Nevertheless, I won't expect you to put it on now. Just know that I'll have it appropriately altered and laundered by tomorrow morning. All I need right now is to take a few quick measurements."

Emma took comfort knowing that she wouldn't need to try on the repugnant robe. "Here is as good a place as any." Emma suggested this, not able to think of a better place and wanting to end the ordeal as fast as possible. "Let's do it."

The tailor worked quickly. First, he held up the robe in front of her, close but a few inches away. Her eyes watered at its mothballed, mildewy stench.

The tailor scanned Emma with a well-practiced eye. Inside, she squirmed at what would be considered an ogle in any other setting, but outside she remained stoic, with a poised indifference.

Laying the robe aside, he then took the needed

measurements, holding his measuring tape close to her without touching her body. He also continued to avoid eye contact.

"This will do," he said within seconds. "I must take my leave and handle the task at hand." He bowed to her again but only slightly so. "My Lord." He paused and bowed again, this time longer and more deeply, as if he judged the first bow to be inadequate. "My Lord." At last, he left.

Emma locked the door behind him, smiling at the thought of Pompous Jack fuming at not being able to walk right in like he owned the place. He didn't, did he? Did that mean she did?

4

THE NOTE

That night Emma twisted in the sprawling bed—her new bed in her new home— trying to find a comfortable position. But sleep escaped her futile efforts. What little rest she got came as interrupted chunks of slumber scattered throughout the night.

The hint of dawn snuck its way into the room, with rays of sunshine slipping around the edges of the heavy drapes. Her eyes popped open, and she jumped out of bed with uncharacteristic early morning perkiness. She showered with excitement, anticipating what this holy day—her first as High Priestess—would bring. She dried her hair and dressed, crinkling her nose as she did. Her stiff clothes reeked.

She checked the time. It wasn't too early. She grabbed her phone, which Captain Hernandez had retrieved and returned sometime during her convalescence. She was glad he was on her side now instead of still trying to arrest her. Grateful for his thoughtfulness, she texted her mom. "Please bring clean clothes."

"Already have them," came the quick reply. "See you soon."

Emma wrinkled her nose. "Can't wait," she texted back.

With a clean body wrapped in dirty clothes, she wondered what to do. She didn't need to wait long.

Someone knocked on the bedroom door. "Breakfast is served, My Lord." The voice was female, likely young.

Emma recoiled once again at the pretentious title but said nothing. She followed the white-clad attendant to a formal dining room with an ample breakfast arranged on one end of an enormous table. The ornate carvings in the rich cherry would impress most people, but it repulsed Emma. In fact, the entire Temple Palace nauseated her. But she shoved that thought aside.

The twenty-something attendant seated Emma

and took a step back, standing rigidly alert with hands clasped before her.

Emma eyed the young woman. "Are you hungry?"

"We attend to ourselves only after everyone else has eaten, My Lord."

"But are you hungry?"

The woman said nothing, though her eyes darted to the food in front of Emma.

"Have a seat." Emma gestured with her head to the chair next to her.

"It wouldn't be proper, My Lord."

"It will be our secret." Emma took a piece of buttered toast off a plate and slid the three remaining slices toward the empty chair. The woman stared at the food. After deliberating what to do, she sat down at last and began to eat, delicately at first and then with more enthusiasm.

"What's your name?"

For the first time, the woman made eye contact with Emma. "Jennifer." She gave a respectful downward tip of her head. "My Lord."

Emma continued to share the abundance of food with Jennifer: juice, fruit, tea, yogurt, waffles, and more. They talked a bit, with Jennifer occasionally lowering her guard but then catching herself and shutting down just as quickly.

Emma whisked a sausage patty off the serving platter and slid the rest to Jennifer.

The young woman stiffened. "With all due respect, My Lord, I must decline. I'm a vegetarian."

Emma froze with her mouth open wide, ready to chomp into her sausage. She dropped her arm to the table. "I'm so sorry. I didn't mean to offend you by eating meat in front of you."

"No offense taken, My Lord," Jennifer said. "Enjoy your food and pay me no mind. But please don't ask me to partake."

"It doesn't seem right to eat meat while you're here."

"Who do you think prepared the sausage?" Jennifer gave Emma a quick wink before regaining her stoic distance.

When they finished eating, Emma stood and began stacking the empty plates and leftover food back on the delivery cart Jennifer had brought.

"Let me do that, My Lord."

"Nonsense," Emma said. "Helping you pick up is the least I can do."

"Thank you, My Lord."

"Please call me Emma. All this 'My Lord' stuff and bowing is driving me crazy."

"As you wish, my . . ." Jennifer smiled for the first time that morning. "It will take some getting used to."

"Perhaps the next day you work, you can deliver my food."

"I work every day."

"Then I look forward to seeing you tomorrow morning, assuming that's on your schedule."

"I work from five in the morning until nine at night, so, yes, it's on my schedule."

"Seriously?"

"We get a break midmorning and again in the afternoon."

"At least you get overtime."

Jennifer shook her head. "They make us donate the extra hours as 'volunteer time' so they don't have to pay us extra."

"They?"

"His Royal Eminence."

"I hope he pays you a nice hourly rate for the rest." Emma wished that to be true, but if Pompous Jack was involved, she suspected not.

"Minimum wage, I'm afraid."

Emma again shook her head. As she thought

about what to say next, a mechanical-sounding alert shot through the room. "What in the world is that?"

"It's a telephone." Jennifer pointed to an appliance sitting in the corner.

Though Emma had never used such a gadget or even seen one in person, she remembered them from old TV shows.

Jennifer scurried over to the device. She picked up a part of it and brought it to her face. "High Priest's residence. This is Jennifer."

Emma walked toward Jennifer to check out this telephone thing.

"No, Your Royal Eminence. She's still here," Jennifer said. "Sorry, sir . . . Yes, sir . . . Right away, sir."

Jennifer lowered the talking part of the device to its cradle and turned toward Emma. "He's in a tizzy that you're not at the auditorium getting ready for today's service. You must leave at once."

"I'm all turned around and don't know how to get there," Emma said. "Will you give me—"

A loud crash reverberated through the Temple Palace. Glass shattered, and a thud shook the floor. Tires squealed.

Emma ran to the source of the noise, with Jennifer close behind. The pair stopped at the doorway to the banquet hall. Broken glass was sprayed around the room. The large picture window, which had been a prominent feature of the space, was now shattered. With a gust of wind, in wafted the ominous smell of gasoline. A brick lay in the middle of the mess with a piece of paper wrapped around it.

"How could this have happened?" Emma wondered aloud. "You'd think there'd be security to keep this from happening."

"My thoughts exactly."

Emma stepped toward the brick, but Jennifer pulled her back.

"You stay here. Let me get it." Tiptoeing around the debris, Jennifer retrieved the offending brick and handed it to Emma.

Emma removed the note, unfolded it, and gasped.

5

THE ROBE

Jennifer moved next to Emma and read the note aloud. "Women shouldn't be priests, especially not High Priests. This is your final warning." She took the note from Emma and slid it into her apron pocket. "You need to get out of here and go to someplace safe. The sanctuary will work for now."

Emma didn't move.

"Now!" Jennifer tugged Emma's arm.

"We should clean this up and make sure there's no fire."

"I'll handle everything," Jennifer said. "We have a protocol for such situations. But I think the gas smell is from the getaway car and not a firebomb."

Jennifer grabbed Emma's wrist and pulled her to a side door. "Follow me."

Once outside, Jennifer took off at a brisk pace, almost jogging, dragging a perplexed Emma behind her, gently but with intention. With ease, Jennifer navigated a series of almost hidden paths and unobtrusive gates. In no time, they reached the side of the auditorium, out of breath but safely away from the peril back at the palace.

"You'll be okay." Jennifer wrapped her arms around Emma and gave her a most-appreciated hug. "Go through this door and turn left. That hall will take you to the side of the sanctuary. I'm sorry, but I must leave you here and follow our terrorist protocol."

Emma pushed the word *terrorist* out of her mind. *Breathe in*, she thought. *Breathe out*. Her panic began to fade. *Thank you, Sovereign, for protecting us. Fill me with your peace and guide Jennifer in what to do.*

Emma faced a small wooden door with peeling gray paint and rusty hinges. It was probably the servants' entrance. Using it suited her just fine. She opened it and entered the massive building.

From there, she walked down the hall. This brought her to the side of the sanctuary, where she took in its cavernous expanse. She and her family typically watched the service on TV from the comfort of their living room—like most families—but they attended in person a few times each year.

Glistening gold—or just gold colored—religious regalia littered the place in every direction. Rich tapestries adorned the walls. Banners from a prior era hung from the ceiling, which an artist of old had covered with impressive images of their history's most revered patriarchs.

Emma was never sure if she should be impressed or repelled by the ornate artwork and ostentatious display of extravagance. She always wondered what the Sovereign thought of such excessiveness. But now she could set her wondering aside and ask the Sovereign directly. The next time they connected, Emma would do just that.

On stage paraded Pompous Jack. He directed a flurry of activity as people fluttered about in frenzied preparation for the service. Yet it wouldn't start for another two hours.

Emma couldn't tell what all the fuss was about, but looking at his face gave her the answer. Pompous Jack beamed with the conceited arrogance of being in charge and having people jump at his command or even his subtlest of gestures.

Hidden in the shadows, no one had yet noticed

her. *Sovereign Lord,* Emma prayed. *May you be pleased with my role in the service today. May your people receive what you want them to receive. Let it be so.*

A surge of peace swelled up in her spirit and eased into her body. She breathed deeply, rolled her shoulders back, and held her head high. She strode toward Pompous Jack with confidence.

When he noticed her, his glow faded. "You're late, little one. Though I'm happy to see you survived your ordeal back at the palace, know that I do not tolerate insubordination."

How does he know about my ordeal? Emma thought. *Jennifer hadn't mentioned it.*

The people nearby grew silent at his reprimand and scurried away. Attempting to recover from his outburst, he forced a pained smile and loudly added, "But not to worry. I have everything under control and have made the needed adjustments."

As attention shifted away from them and activity resumed, anger flashed from Pompous Jack's eyes. He grabbed Emma's shoulder and jerked her toward him, crinkling his nose as she came closer. With a firm grip, he shoved her to his left. "The last door on the left is your dressing room." He pushed her toward it. "Get in there, now. My team is waiting to make you look presentable." He glared at her until she edged toward the door. As she moved away, his countenance rebounded, and he returned his focus to other preparations.

Emma reached the last door. It felt proper to knock, yet, if this was her dressing room, she should just walk in like she owned the place. Maybe she did. She was High Priestess, after all.

Inside, two people awaited her. One was the tailor from yesterday. The other was an attractive young woman, perhaps only a couple of years older than her.

The tailor spoke first. "I've altered and laundered your robe. It will serve you adequately for today, My Lord. A much more appropriate vestment will await you next week." He held out this ugliest of all garments for Emma.

Gross! She took it from him. *So gross.* But there was no use taking out her frustration on him. "Thank you for your extra work on short notice. I really appreciate it." Her words sounded almost grown-up, and she wondered if she was losing herself in this new role as High Priestess.

Emma studied the robe to decide if she should pull it over her head or step into it. She looked to the tailor for direction, but he had turned his back to her. So had the young woman.

Emma assumed this was to give her privacy. Awkwardly, she pulled it over her head and shimmied her shoulders to make it fall into place. "How's this?" She gestured with her arms, marveling at the grossly oversized sleeves that drooped below them. The weight of the garment shocked her. Moving fast or with ease wouldn't happen.

The tailor turned and clicked his tongue with a hint of disapproval. "The priests remove their outer garments before donning a robe."

"You mean they're in their underwear?" An amused giggle sneaked out of Emma's mouth. She'd never look at a priest in his robe the same way.

"Precisely, My Lord." The tailor's face softened. "It keeps them from overheating."

"I feel much more comfortable keeping my clothes on."

"As you wish, My Lord," the tailor said as he lowered his head in reverence. "Please raise the cowl. I want to ensure it fits properly."

Emma complied. The oversized hood had almost as much extra material as her sleeves. She laughed. It hung over her head and hid much of her face.

"Oh my," the tailor said. "It's too small. I seem to have removed too much fabric."

"It seems too big to me."

"It's supposed to be even bigger. Oh, my. What to do?" He gave the hood a firm tug forward, which pulled tightly on the back of Emma's head and produced even more material to flutter in front of her face. "This will have to do for today, My Lord. Please forgive my miscalculation."

"No worries," Emma said. "It's all good."

"Then I will take my leave and let the two of you get to work." He gestured toward the young woman and looked back at Emma. "I'll watch everything online. It's much too stressful to be here in person."

"I get that."

He lowered his voice. "Plus, if I'm not here, His Royal Eminence can't yell at me."

The tailor scurried away.

6

MAKEUP

Emma glanced at the young woman, judging her to be about eighteen or nineteen. She wore pull-on, black slacks and a loose-fitting, white smock, which bore the name of Ashley, written in a flowery script.

Like everyone Emma had met here in the last two days, Ashley avoided eye contact. She gave Emma a slight bow. "I'm Ashley, My Lord, and I'm here to do your makeup."

"Please call me Emma. That's what my friends do."

"I could never presume, My Lord."

"Will you try?" Emma asked. "For my sake?"

Ashley didn't answer Emma's question and gestured toward an upright chair. "Please have a seat and remove that disgusting hood." She shuddered. "Forgive my impudence, My Lord . . . I mean my Emma. It's just that I don't want to get makeup on it."

"I think it's hideous too. Don't worry, I'm not planning on using it."

"That may not be wise, my . . . Emma."

A soft knock on the door ended the discussion. "I hope it's my mom with clean clothes. I've been wearing this same outfit since Thursday morning." Emma rushed to the door as fast as her robe allowed, and she let her mom in. They hugged each other tightly, even though they had just seen each other yesterday.

"I had to do some fast talking to get past His Royal Eminence," Mom said. "And I had to promise to leave right away."

"I'm glad you didn't cave," Emma said. "Is the fam here? Will you stay for the service?" Emma knew the answers to both questions. "If you want, we can eat here afterward and then go home."

Emma's mom agreed, handed Emma her clothes, and hurried away, no doubt wanting to avoid Pompous Jack's wrath.

"You're going home after the service?" Ashley raised her eyebrows.

"That's my plan, but let's keep that between the two of us."

"Agreed."

Emma threw back the hood and sat in the chair for Ashley. Though Emma didn't normally wear makeup—her mom insisted she looked beautiful without any—she anticipated what Ashley might come up with. The young woman opened the largest makeup kit Emma had ever seen and went to work arranging selected creams, powders, and brushes on the table.

"I went to cosmetology school as I finished up high school," Ashley said as she applied foundation. "Good thing your skin is clean because we don't have time for a cleanse—I graduated from both a year ago June and started working here right away. I was homeschooled, so it was no problem at all to do both. Homeschool in the morning and cosmetology in the afternoon. Easy peasy—we're also skipping mascara and eyeliner—public schools waste so much time. So doing both was no problem—close your eyes a sec—never dreamed I could do cosmetology and work for the Sovereign at the same time, but here I am, My Lord. I mean my Emma."

Emma opened her mouth to respond, but Ashley interrupted with more words and a vigorous dusting of a light-colored powder. Emma snapped her eyes shut just in time.

"Oh no. Please forgive me for rambling. I talk when I get nervous. And being around you makes me really, really, really nervous. But it's good too. For the past year, it's only been guys. I cut hair, trim beards, and give morning shaves. And there's an occasional perm for His Royal Eminence. I do makeup on Sunday morning for those who will be on camera. But it's all men. That is, until you came. Until today. I'm so jazzed about doing your makeup, even if it's not what I had in mind. This is the best day of my life. Seriously. Oh no, here I go again—rambling."

As Ashley caught her breath from her rapid-fire monologue, Emma jumped in. "Don't be nervous, Ashley. I'm a girl, just like you. Treat me like a friend."

"That will be hard for me to do, my Emma."

"From what I've seen, you're the closest one here to my age. Us girls need to stick together. To be friends."

"I haven't had the time to make friends here," Ashley said. "They keep us pretty busy."

"Let me guess. Long hours, seven days a week, no personal time."

"That sums it up. And when I'm not doing hair and makeup, I have to help food services because they're short-staffed and have too much work."

"There's a guy here that you like," Emma said. "Am I right?" Emma knew this to be true but chastised herself for blurting it out when she had no reason to.

"His name is Topher," Ashley gushed. Her face beamed. "But how did you know?"

How indeed? Lately these impertinent questions kept popping out of Emma's mouth before she had a chance to think. But each one revealed something important. Was the Sovereign's Divine Spirit prompting her words? This was another consideration to ponder.

"Topher's a nice name," Emma said. "Tell me about him."

"First of all, he's easy on the eyes." Ashley's dimples popped. "He's the palace chauffeur. He works hard, is kind to everyone, and is a man of integrity. More importantly, we're at the same place spiritually—at least I think so." Her face lit up, and she exhaled a contented sigh, patting her chest three times. "Just thinking about him makes my little heart go pitter-patter." Her eyes misted a bit, which she chased away with several fluttering blinks.

"You two dating?"

"Oh, no!" Ashley exclaimed. "We're not allowed to be in a relationship with coworkers. Though I'm sure he likes me, too, we have to admire each other from a distance."

"You can't date?"

"His Royal Eminence prohibits fraternization."

"That's not right," Emma said. "I don't remember reading that in the Holy Text."

Ashley dropped her hands as the makeup brush rattled to the floor. She stared at Emma, mouth agape. "You read the Holy Text?"

"For sure. I've not read everything yet, but I seriously doubt that the Sovereign prohibits Temple employees from dating and marrying."

Ashley didn't respond. Instead, she picked up the brush and applied some final flourishes to Emma's cheeks. Taking a step back, she surveyed her work. "It's certainly not my choice, but it's exactly what His Royal Eminence demanded. He should be pleased—even if I'm not." She handed Emma a mirror.

The ghostly image that stared back appalled Emma, but she did her best to not react. "This is what he *told* you to do?" She couldn't bring herself to call him His Royal Eminence, and she needed to keep her nickname of Pompous Jack to herself.

"Yes, His Royal Eminence said to de-emphasize all your prominent features and give you an ethereal look."

"Well, you certainly did an excellent job," Emma said.

Take a picture, the Sovereign whispered in Emma's mind.

"Let's document your work with a selfie," Emma said aloud to Ashley.

Ashley pulled out her phone but hesitated.

Emma nestled up next to her. "Let's do two. The first serious and the other fun. Text them to me."

7

SUNDAY SERVICE

Now that Ashley was gone, Emma had a few moments to herself. With haste, she removed the robe, changed into the clean clothes her mom had brought, and worked to remove the ghostly makeup, restoring her pure, youthful glow. The selfie would provide Ashley with proof that she'd done exactly what Pompous Jack instructed and protect her from his certain reprisals.

Emma pulled the ostentatious robe back on just as someone knocked on the door. "Please report to the platform, High Priestess. The people have gathered. Cameras roll in five."

"Be right there," Emma said. She pulled the cowl over her head, suddenly glad for the cover the extra material afforded her. If she kept her head tipped down, Pompous Jack might not see she had removed her makeup until it was too late.

She moved toward the stage, her head lowered in reverence.

"Follow me to the platform," Pompous Jack hissed without looking at her. "I'll sit in the cathedra, and you sit in the smaller chair next to it. You will receive two cues to say your two lines. Don't mess this up."

"No problem," Emma said.

Keeping her head down, she followed him and sat on the tiny chair next to his.

Her years of stage experience prepared her for what was about to happen. Though her audiences had always been small, today was different. For her, today would be a performance for an audience of one—the Sovereign—with everyone else being mere observers.

People packed the sanctuary, and many stood in the back. Emma had never seen this many people here. At best it would be half full for special occasions. Usually, a small fraction of that showed up on any given Sunday.

In no time, the stage director gave the countdown to going live. He held up five fingers, then four, three, two, one. He pointed at the chorister, who led the chancel choir to the stage. They sang an opening number. The somber song overshadowed an accomplished vocal performance. When they finished, the choir parted, each half moving to one side of the stage. The director gave Emma her first cue.

She rose and, with her head down, eased to the podium. Inside, she shook with nervous energy, but outside, she gave off a calm, confident vibe as she glided forward. Thousands were watching in person and millions more would watch online. It didn't matter to her, not until an unexpected heat rushed through her body. A surge of panic struck. This robe was too hot, and she must do something about it—fast—before she fainted.

Having arrived at her mark, Emma looked up for the first time and surveyed those who had gathered. They stared at her with expectation, some eyes worried she would fail and others shining with hopeful anticipation.

She raised her arms to her head and grasped the sides of her hood, slowly pushing it back. This released the oppressive heat it had corralled around her head. A refreshing coolness bathed her face and restored the calm that the robe had threatened to boil away.

Several people gasped. Though most in the audience smiled their approval, a few recoiled in horror. No one had ever seen an officiant with their hood lowered. But the sensation of the Sovereign's approval soothed her soul, and that's what mattered. She didn't care if some viewed her act as sacrilegious.

She fixed her eyes on a most pleasant and supportive-looking lady who stood in the back. As if speaking to that woman only, Emma dramatically stretched out her arms on each side. The baggy sleeves gave off a grand appearance. Of this, she was sure.

Now she was ready to deliver her one line. "Welcome to today's service." Emma smiled, surveyed the room, and returned to her seat. Pompous Jack eyed her, but he was in no position to communicate his anger or offer correction, lest the cameras document his displeasure. She was safe. For now.

The choir sang three more numbers and left the stage. Now it was Pompous Jack's turn to go through the prescribed rituals. Watching these religious ceremonies in person and on TV had always filled Emma with a feeling of sanctified awe, but viewing them from behind left her underwhelmed.

Of course, she couldn't shake from her mind the fact that under Pompous Jack's ostentatious robe was nothing but his tighty-whities.

Emma had plenty of experience remaining on stage for long periods as a secondary character, waiting for her next cue. She painted a pleased look of approval on her face and allowed her mind to go elsewhere. She thought of Joshua, wondering if she would ever see him again. Had the captain fulfilled her request to release all the other prisoners? What about Mrs. Butler, her missing religion teacher? Everyone assumed she'd been arrested for heresy.

Emma thought about what Ashley had said about Topher. That he was easy on the eyes, a hard worker, and a kind man with integrity. Joshua checked all those boxes. They were also going in the same direction spiritually. Of that, she was sure. But even though she had wondered what it would be like to kiss him, he didn't make her heart go pitter-patter—whatever that meant. This loomed as a huge con on her much longer list of pros. Should she try to think of him only as a friend and nothing more? Was that even possible?

The choir left the stage after concluding their last song, bringing Emma's mind back to the present. The director cued her, and she approached the lectern, this time smiling and with head held high. She reached her mark and gave a dramatic pause as she surveyed the crowd. Capturing their attention, no one moved. Quiet pervaded the place.

"Thank you for attending today's service." She had said her prescribed line, but she didn't feel she was done. She raised her right arm high with her palm facing the congregation. "May the Sovereign bless all that you do as you travel through this week." She lowered her hand and prepared to exit the stage, but an impetuous impulse kept her where she was. She grinned and waved at the crowd. "See you next Sunday!"

As one, the congregants rose to their feet and applauded.

Their approval fueled her satisfaction. With a confident stride, she exited the stage, all the while wondering what sort of rage Pompous Jack would rain down on her.

8

THE AFTERMATH

Emma headed toward her dressing room, carrying the elixir of the people's applause with her. She willed herself to hold on to this memory—something to sustain her in what was surely about to happen. Before she could reach her destination, however, a firm hand grabbed her shoulder and spun her around. It was Pompous Jack. He glared daggers at her.

"Get your hand off me," Emma said, "and don't you dare ever touch me again."

"I can't begin to list all the ways you disappointed me and disrespected today's service," Pompous Jack said. "You can't follow directions, and you almost started a riot. And I'm going to fire that insubordinate twit of a makeup girl."

"First of all, Ashley did exactly what you told her to do. She has a picture to prove it. I removed the makeup. And I followed your directions exactly, responding to my cues and saying the two lines you told me to say. As far as a riot, I'd hardly call a standing ovation a riot."

"You'll pay for what you did, you impertinent child."

"Is that any way to speak to your High Priestess?" Emma spun around, leaving a stunned Pompous Jack in her wake as she retreated to her dressing room. She jerked the door closed and set the lock.

She'd already peeled off her robe and tossed it over the back of a chair, when Pompous Jack pounded on her door. "Let me in, you ingrate, you spoiled child." The knob on the door jangled, but the lock held firm. Pompous Jack beat the door again. "This isn't over, you little brat. I'll be back to deal with you and put an end to your rebellious spirit."

Emma refused to let her emotions take over or to release her frustration with tears. Instead, she forced out a breath, sending with it the tension that his tirade had roiled up inside her. She peeked under the door to make sure he wasn't lurking outside. After counting to ten to make sure he was gone, she scooted out and darted to the vestibule. Her family waited. Their broad smiles told her they approved, that they affirmed what she had done.

"You were amazing," her dad said.

"We couldn't be prouder," Mom added.

"Awesome sauce!" said Hailey.

All eyes turned to Brayden. "At least you didn't screw it up."

Emma ruffled his hair before he could squirm away. "Love you, too, bro." She returned her gaze to her parents. "Thank you for being here. Your support means a lot to me. Who's hungry?" She gestured toward the exit. Everyone turned, and she slid in between her parents, linking her arms with theirs.

They entered the Temple Palace through the servants' door in back. The most delightful smells greeted them. They walked to the dining room, where Jennifer scurried to set the table. Four carts of food lined the back wall.

"You arrived sooner than I expected. My sincerest apologies. It will only take me a few more minutes," Jennifer said, making a stiff bow. "By the way, I caught the service online. You were brilliant."

Emma slid up to Jennifer and laid a hand on

hers to calm the harried server's preparations. "Don't stress. It's all good."

Jennifer paused and blinked back the weight of her emotions.

"I'd like you to meet the fam."

Jennifer turned to face them, shoulders back and standing straight.

"Mom, Dad, this is my new friend Jennifer. Jennifer, this is my mother, Liz, my father, Zack, and the twins, Hailey and Brayden."

"I'm the older one." Hailey waved and beamed.

"But I'm the faster one," Brayden said as he jumped in front of his sister.

After her parents exchanged greetings with Jennifer, Emma helped her set out the food. With five places already arranged around the end of the long table, Emma pulled up a sixth chair and placed it next to her for Jennifer.

Everyone sat down, and Emma gave the opening blessing. The sound of her "amen" unleashed a flurry of activity as everyone piled Jennifer's bounty on their plates. This Sunday feast was just like back home—except with much more food. And Jennifer fit right in, like she was part of Emma's family.

For a time, Emma forgot her confrontation with Pompous Jack and the brick that was thrown through the window only a few hours before.

To wrap up the meal, Emma's mom gave the concluding prayer. Everyone helped pick up. Soon, they had all the dishes and leftover food loaded on the four carts.

Emma gave Jennifer a grateful hug. "Thank you for a wonderful meal," she said. Lowering her voice, she added, "And for getting everything from this morning cleaned up so quickly."

Jennifer whispered back, "That's why we have a response protocol in place. We've notified the authorities, and they're investigating. So, don't you worry."

Emma turned to her parents. "Shall we head home?"

"Is that wise?" her mom asked.

"No problem," Emma said.

"What am I to tell His Royal Eminence when he asks where you are?" Jennifer asked.

"Tell him the truth. I was here when you left."

Jennifer pushed one cart and pulled another one to the service entrance. Emma handled the other two. Once they maneuvered all four carts outside,

Emma watched her friend push two of the carts toward the primary kitchen back at the cafeteria.

Then Emma left with her family out the front door.

9

DO YOU TRUST ME?

On Monday morning Emma knocked on Chloe's back door fifteen minutes ahead of schedule. No response. Emma rapped again, this time harder. Soon, footfalls reverberated from inside and grew closer.

Chloe peeked out. A foaming toothbrush stuck out of her mouth. "You' ea'ly."

"Sorry. But I want to talk to you about something important before school."

Chloe held up her index finger. "'e 'ight 'ack." She scampered away.

Emma walked inside and waited for her friend to return.

Soon, a bright-eyed Chloe reemerged, accompanied by the scent of fresh mint toothpaste. "I can't believe the High Priestess is in my house."

"I'm still Emma, and we're still BFFs. That will never change."

"Ah, okay." But Chloe looked doubtful. "What's up, BFF?"

"Do you trust me?" Emma asked.

"What kind of question is that?"

"Have I ever done anything to hurt you?"

"No." Chloe gathered her black hair behind her head and corralled it into a short ponytail. "Spill."

"I want to try something, but in case it doesn't work, I don't want you to think I'm crazy."

"Should I be scared or excited?"

Emma extended her hands in front of her, palms up. "Give me your hands."

Hesitating for only a moment, Chloe laid her hands on Emma's.

"Close your eyes. Open your mind to receive."

Chloe's eyelids fluttered shut.

"As we read in the Holy Text," Emma said, "I impart to you the Sovereign's Divine Spirit to—"

Chloe jerked her hands back, her eyes popped open, and she sucked in a deep breath. "Holy moly!" She fell backward to the floor with a thud.

Preparing to apologize, Emma reached out to help her friend stand, but Chloe didn't move.

"Incredible!" Joy beamed from Chloe's face. Her aura glowed in the spiritual realm. A faint, lime green light shone from Chloe's essence. Tears rolled down her cheeks.

Emma plopped onto the floor next to her astonished friend. "This is what I should've told you about. This is what I want you to experience."

"Clarity," Chloe said. "Complete clarity. Everything makes sense. You. The Sovereign. Life." A final tear leaked from Chloe's right eye. "I guess you gave me my birthday present early."

Emma wrapped her arms around Chloe and pulled her close.

It took several minutes before Chloe tried to stand. Even then, she was a bit wobbly. "I'm not sure what just happened, but suddenly school doesn't seem so important."

"We should go anyway," Emma said this even though she agreed with Chloe. Emma had to cling to her old life lest she lose herself in this new role as High Priestess. "Let's get moving, so we're not late."

Joshua waited on the sidewalk in front of Chloe's house. "Joshua!" Emma shrieked. She ran to him with open arms and gave him a ginormous hug. "You're free."

"You made it happen." Joshua pulled back a bit and planted a quick kiss on her forehead.

Emma looked up into his glorious, brown eyes, wondering if a kiss on the lips would follow. Afraid that it wouldn't but hoping it would, she held her breath, her pulse raced. This would be her first real kiss—ever. The kiss she had dreamed of and that the Sovereign had teased her about.

Joshua's gaze met hers. He bent to her level as she raised to her tiptoes. He leaned his head to the side and moved his lips toward hers. Her heart thumped, and she closed her eyes. Their lips touched for the briefest of moments. Excitement surged through Emma's body. Her heart tingled, but her lips froze. They refused to work and didn't kiss him back.

Joshua tensed. He dropped his embrace and pulled back. Looking at the ground, he cleared his throat. "I guess we should head to school." He turned and walked away, leaving Emma standing there in wide-eyed horror.

Mortified over what she had just done—of what she didn't do—Emma watched him stride away.

Embarrassment replaced her short-lived exhilaration.

Chloe slid alongside her. "Shake it off, girlfriend." Chloe hooked her arm with Emma's and urged the trembling girl forward. "If it's meant to be, you'll have many more chances."

Emma took a tentative step forward to follow Joshua. *Breathe in,* she thought. *Breathe out.* The Sovereign's peace filled her.

The pair caught up with Joshua. "Scoot over, dude," Chloe said.

Joshua moved to the side of the walk, and Chloe guided Emma forward next to him. The three moved toward school, side by side by side. A tinge of hopefulness entered Emma's soul and pushed away her embarrassment over her epic failure at her first kiss.

Lane soon joined them. "Sorry I'm late. In case you haven't heard," he said playfully, "we got a new High Priestess this weekend. It's been kind of distracting."

Emma ignored his comment. She yearned for this Monday to be like every other one, but it seemed no one was going to let that happen.

As they traveled their path toward school, they

picked up their friends along the way. Amazed, Emma saw that in the spiritual realm, each one of them—all twelve—had a color. But aside from her, Chloe, and Joshua—none of them had an aura. At least not yet.

Emma resolved to change that. As far as she knew, it was just the three of them and Gabe who had the Sovereign's Divine Spirit in them.

She wondered if indeed they might be her disciples, but she pushed that thought away. The idea was too much for her to deal with today.

As the school came into view, Gabe stood on the sidewalk as if waiting for her. Instead of wearing his usual tattered, once-white robe, he sported blue jeans, a flannel shirt, and tennis shoes. Aside from his flowing white mane and straggly gray beard, he looked almost normal.

Chloe shook her head. "There's something about him that unsettles me."

"He's a good man," Emma said. "And most wise. He has much to teach us."

"You're probably right," Chloe said. "But there's something about him I can't put my finger on."

Emma stopped and turned to her cadre—her disciples—who trailed along behind. "You guys go on. I need to talk to my friend for a moment."

10

—————

NOT THE ONE

After the troupe passed her and headed to school, Emma strode up to Gabe. "You messed up, old man. You said I wasn't the One." She couldn't hide the smirk on her face.

"But you aren't."

"Haven't you heard? Over the weekend I became High Priestess. Totally unexpected."

Gabe let out a chortle. "Forgive my lack of specificity and permit me to offer elucidation. When I said you weren't the One, I referred to the One of whom the prophets foretold. Since you said you read the Holy Text, I assumed you possessed a working knowledge about their prognostications."

The smirk left Emma's face. "I haven't gotten to

the prophetic part yet." She dropped her head. "Just the history and wisdom sections."

"Irrespective of your current standing as High Priestess, I can confirm that you are not and will never be the One." Now it was Gabe's turn to fidget. "But I would like to offer a slight correction. When I said you *are* close to the One, I should have said that you *will* be close to the One."

"Is it Joshua? Sarah?"

"Though both worthy candidates, neither will be the One. Joshua, however, will one day be close as well."

"Am I supposed to understand this?" Emma asked.

"When the necessity to comprehend the meaning of my words comes to be, then—and only then—will everything come into focus."

"Great," Emma said. "That's not much help."

"I was quite astonished this morning when the Sovereign told me to meet you here and that you'd be arriving on foot," Gabe said. "I am most surprised that Pompous Jack let you leave."

"He didn't. I escaped," Emma said. "And how do you know my nickname for him? I never told you—or anyone, for that matter."

"As you may recall, the Sovereign permits our

thoughts to connect, in what you wrongly label as telepathy. But only when you will it to happen does my access to your mind not encounter barriers."

"But I didn't do that." Emma cocked her head to the side and glared.

"Last night, as you immersed yourself in prayer, you petitioned the Sovereign for us to connect. Though I suspect you expected it to transpire today in our physical reality, it occurred at that precise moment in the spiritual realm."

"I'll need to be more careful."

"As the Holy Text instructs, 'Take hold of every thought and subject it to your will.' We only had the briefest of connections. When your thoughts shifted to young Joshua, you blocked my access."

Emma gave this a test. *How many other people has the Sovereign allowed you to communicate with like this?* Emma asked through her thoughts.

You are the first, Gabe thought in response.

The first? You act like you do this all the time.

I have long considered it as a supernatural possibility, but I never experienced my theory as reality until you came along.

What about Joshua? Emma thought. *Does the Sovereign allow you to connect with his mind as well?*

I suspect master Joshua will be the second.

Emma changed the subject. "By the way, I like your new look and your lack of a . . . scent."

"I'm residing for a time at master Joshua and Sarah's abode. Their mother gifted me with food and a hot shower. Despite three futile attempts, however, she failed to launder my robe to her satisfaction. That relic of what I once was is no more. She afforded me two changes of her husband's unused garments."

Emma's phone vibrated, alerting her that she had five minutes to get to her first class. "I need to go. We'll talk more—soon." She jogged toward the main entrance to the school.

As she entered the building, an unexpected announcement blasted over the PA system. It was Principal Johnson. "Attention all students. Attention all students. The High Priestess has entered the building. Please clear the halls immediately and give her clear passage. I repeat, please clear the halls immediately."

11

PRINCIPAL JOHNSON

Emma detoured into the reception area of the school office. At first, no one noticed her. She cleared her throat. "May I speak to Principal Johnson?" All work stopped and their eyes turned toward her then looked away just as quickly.

Principal Johnson emerged from his private office. He tipped his head toward her. It signified respect without yielding authority. "Perhaps we should meet in my office, My Lord. Your presence here is disrupting the staff from their work." With eyes averted, he gestured toward his open office door.

Emma walked in and plopped onto the seat in front of his desk. He followed but stood stiffly in the doorway. Now it was her turn to gesture, and she motioned toward his desk chair.

"Yes, My Lord." He pulled the door shut and sat. Taking his glasses off, he laid them on his desk and rubbed his eyes.

Though Emma looked at him, he didn't return her gaze. "Please, call me Emma. Just like you did last week. I'm the same girl now as I was then."

"Though you may feel like the same person, with all due respect, you are now quite different. You are, in fact, the High Priestess—the spiritual head of our country and the Divine's representative to the entire world."

"I just want to go to school and graduate without any fuss."

"I'm afraid that's not a realistic option anymore. This morning, I contacted His Royal Eminence and offered to send a tutor to the palace to continue your education, but it seems that . . . he lost you." At last, Principal Johnson glanced at her, a hint of a smile playing on his lips. "It is the best solution for all concerned. You saw firsthand the disruption your presence caused with my office staff. Multiply that by each class you are in and every time you walk the halls."

"Just let me try. Give me one week."

Principal Johnson shook his head slowly. He opened his mouth to speak, but Emma spoke first.

"And so that everyone else can switch classes without me 'being a distraction,'" she said, making quote marks with her fingers, "what if my teachers let me leave three minutes before the end of class, so I can be at my next one before the bell rings?"

"Against my better judgment, I will grant you one week. But do not let your presence here inhibit learning from taking place or turn this school into a circus. If you do, High Priestess or not, I'll insist you leave."

Emma stood. "Deal." She extended her right hand to shake his.

He stood but didn't reciprocate her gesture. "I accept your proposal. Now hurry to class so that we can release everyone else to go to theirs."

Emma hustled to her locker. A note slid out when she opened the door. She unfolded the paper to read its message. "You don't belong here, and we don't want you. This is your final warning."

Shoving the threat into her pocket, she grabbed her books and scooted into her first hour class. Her flustered teacher forced a fake smile and picked up her phone. "She's here. You can release everyone else."

"Attention all students," Principal Johnson boomed over the PA system. "The halls are now clear. All students report immediately to your first hour class."

As each student walked into the room, they noticed Emma, looked away, and sat as far from her as they could. No one talked. When the bell rang for them to start class, the teacher stood, her face pale. Her lips quivered, and her hands shook.

Bravely, the teacher opened with a message for the students, one carefully thought out but timidly delivered. "As we are all aware, our country welcomed a new High Priestess this past weekend. And to our utter surprise, she's sitting in this class. We must push this fact aside, however, and work hard to continue to pursue learning. It's important we not let her presence distract us from the task at hand. She has asked us to treat her as we always have. Let us strive to honor her request to the best of our abilities."

The teacher launched into her lesson but struggled to communicate its essential elements. Aside from Emma, no one in the class made any effort to answer the teacher's questions or engage in discussion.

The next two classes unfolded with the same

awkwardness. Lunch was the worst, and Emma ended up eating outside and away from everyone else. Chloe joined her and soon so did Joshua, but an unspoken tension walled between them. The kiss that he offered, and that she bungled, weighed on her heavily, but she dared not say anything about it.

At last, this most dreadful of all days ended, and Emma hoped that tomorrow would go better, but she doubted it would.

Sovereign, Lord, she prayed, *I don't know if I can deal with much more of this. Why is this so hard? I just want to give up. Why aren't you helping me more?*

I never told you it would be easy. The Sovereign's words formed in Emma's mind. *Just trust me to provide what you need, day by day. These trials will make you stronger, preparing you for the powerful woman you are to become. As long as you seek me and put me first in all things, I will never fail or abandon you.*

Emma wanted to do just that and trust the Sovereign, but she wondered if she could. Maybe the Sovereign had made a mistake in picking her to be High Priestess.

12

HANDS

After the final bell, Emma led her cadre away from school and safely to their homes. Though she didn't think anyone else sensed the awkward tension between her and Joshua, it rumbled in her gut like a gulp of sour milk. Once she dropped Chloe off at her house, it was just Emma and Joshua.

At last, he addressed the tension between them. "I'm sorry for trying to kiss you this morning."

"I'm not. Next time I'll do better."

"So . . . we're all good?"

"Hope so."

As the two resumed walking toward Emma's house, she allowed the back of her hand to dangle next to his. Their hands bumped into each other.

They brushed. As if being of one mind, their hands wrapped around each other. Their fingers intertwined.

And Emma's heart went pitter-patter.

They strolled toward her house in silence. But Joshua interrupted her bliss.

"Gee, I can't believe I'm holding hands with the High Priestess."

"Ew! Gross. No, you're not. You're holding hands with Emma Barlow. Don't you ever forget that."

Joshua's frame stiffened a bit, and he was quiet for several seconds. At last, he spoke. "Got it."

Emma tipped her head and leaned against him. Like air escaping from a balloon, the tension in his body released. He let go of her hand and wrapped his arm around her shoulder, pulling her close.

She countered by extending her arm around his waist, pulling him even tighter. Aside from family, she'd never been this close to another person, especially a boy. Excitement surged through her body like a magic elixir. This, most certainly, would be the highlight of her day—a moment she hoped to never forget.

But her euphoria was short-lived.

They rounded the corner to an unexpected

sight. In front of her house sat a white limousine parked perfectly at the curb. In the driveway sat her dad's and mom's cars, even though they never got home from work this early.

"Something's up," Emma said, "and I don't think it's good."

"Should I leave?" Joshua pulled away from Emma and she let him, as though what they were doing was wrong.

"Please don't." She looked up at his face, searching for a clue about what he was thinking. "Unless you want to, that is."

"I'll stay. Until you tell me to go."

"Good answer." She reached for his hand and squeezed it.

He reciprocated. "I've got your back—always have."

Their pace slowed as they made their way to her front door. They entered with hesitation.

There sat Pompous Jack in the living room. Her parents and the sibs sat arrayed around him, engrossed with what he was saying. When he saw them, his broad smile left him.

Pompous Jack stood, glancing at Joshua with disapproval before he strode toward Emma and wrapped his arms around her. "Oh, my dear

Emma." He hugged her tightly, edging Joshua away in the process. "I'm so relieved to see you and over-joyed that you are safe. We have all been quite worried."

"I told you to never touch me again," Emma hissed in his ear. "Get your hands off me. Now."

He patted her shoulder three times. "Seeing you safe and sound fills me with much joy."

She brought her left hand, the one no one could see, to his side just above his hip. Using her thumb and forefinger, she pinched at his shirt, seeking to grab a bit of his skin too. She applied as much force as she could, pressing her thumbnail into her finger.

"Ouch!" Pompous Jack dropped his embrace as if his skin were burning. He pulled back, rubbing his side with vigor.

Everyone stared at him.

"Muscle spasm . . . It should pass in a moment." Pompous Jack rubbed his side as he returned to his chair.

But before he could sit, Emma's dad rose. "If you will excuse us for a moment, Emma's mother and I would like to have a private conversation with our daughter."

The twins bolted upstairs, and Pompous Jack headed toward the front door. Joshua didn't move until Emma tipped her head to signal it was okay. He followed Pompous Jack outside, where Emma hoped her friend would wait.

Once the three of them were safely alone, Emma rushed toward her dad and gave him an enormous hug, which they expanded to include her mom. "I don't know what that man has been telling you, but don't believe a single word he said."

"Emma," her dad said, "you've been through a lot in the last few days . . . perhaps you're misreading the situation."

Emma pulled back from her parents. "I assure you, I am not."

"Why don't we all sit," her dad said, "and we can talk."

"He's not to be trusted."

"Speaking of trust," her dad said, "you shouldn't have snuck off with us on Sunday, letting us assume you received his permission."

"I don't need his permission to do anything. I just needed to get away from him. He's trying to control me, use me for his agenda."

"Honey," her mom said, "he only wants what's in your best interest."

"No, Mother." Emma's face tightened. "He only wants what's in *his* best interest."

"Given all that's happened, your father and I agree you need to live at the Temple Palace. It's not what we want, but it's the only practical solution."

Emma flashed a doubtful glare, cocked her head to the side, and stood, planting a fist on each hip. "I can't believe you're taking his side."

"We're not taking sides," her dad said. "We're being realistic. You can't live here and go to school, pretending like nothing's happened."

"Then come live at the Temple Palace with me! There's a ton of space."

Her parents flashed a glance at each other and in a silent second reached their conclusion.

"As tempting as that is, it wouldn't be fair to the twins." Her dad's words came out slow, measured, and final. "We want to give them as much of a chance as possible to live a normal life, given that their sister is the new High Priestess and all."

"Will you at least think about it?"

"You can't ignore the fact that you're on track to be our country's next spiritual leader," her mom said, shaking her head.

"Even though I didn't want the job and am not ready for it—and doubt I ever will be—I'm already in that role. I just need someone to guide me and keep me from being totally overwhelmed. But that man"—she thrust her arm toward the door—"is not the one." A gleam formed on her face. "I'm going to fire him the first chance I get."

"You can do that?" Her mom raised an eyebrow.

"I don't know, but it sure felt good to say." Emma drew in a slow breath. She needed to control the emotions swirling within her. She willed herself not to cry. That luxury would have to wait until later, once she was alone.

"I'll do whatever you tell me to do," Emma said at last, "even if it's not what I want."

"It's not what we want either," her mom said. "But we think you need to return with His Royal Eminence and live in the High Priest's residence at the Temple Palace."

"Starting tonight," her dad added.

13

HER LAST DINNER

"Can I at least eat dinner here tonight with you and the sibs?" Emma asked her parents. "And can Joshua stay too —assuming he's still here? But no one else."

"I think dinner tonight is a grand idea." Her mom stood. "Let me see what I can throw together."

"And it will give us a chance to meet this Joshua," her dad added. "Why haven't you told us about him? You know we'd have been supportive."

"Sorry, but it's been a more recent thing. Kind of like, as of today."

"Shall I explain the situation to His Royal Eminence?" her dad asked. "And invite Joshua to stay?"

"Thanks, but I'll deal with it. It's what a good High Priestess would do. And what a good girlfriend would do." Emma smiled. *I have a boyfriend.*

She found Joshua and Pompous Jack squirming on the front step outside the house, one on each side of the front door. With arms crossed, they glared at each other in an uneasy standoff. Neither said a word.

Emma flashed Joshua a quick smile and then turned to Pompous Jack. "I'm going to stay here for dinner. You can go back to the Temple. Please send the limo for me in three hours, and I'll return willingly." She extended her smallest finger. "Pinky swear."

Pompous Jack rolled his eyes at her, even as his pinky touched hers for the briefest of moments. With a huff, he turned and marched to the limo.

Emma turned to Joshua and invited him to stay for dinner. He said yes. As they watched the limo disappear, their hands bumped into each other, and their fingers intertwined.

"That man is evil," Joshua said. "Complete evil."

"So right." Emma was glad that Joshua knew this. "But my parents don't see it, so let's not mention it during dinner."

"Got it."

"Let's go inside and talk with my dad. I'm sure he wants to grill you." Emma flashed Joshua her best smile and gave him what she hoped was a playful wink. "No worries. He's a great dad. I'm sure you two will get along just fine. After all, you have me in common."

14

GOING HOME

After dinner, Emma's dad and Joshua cleared the table and washed dishes while Emma and her mom headed to her room to pack some clothes.

"I think your dad's in love." Emma's mom smirked. "At last, he has someone to talk soccer with."

"They seemed to hit it off."

Emma reached her bedroom door and stopped short. Her mom bumped into her. There, on her dresser, sat the largest bouquet of red roses she'd ever seen.

"Oh, I completely forgot," her mom said. "They were sitting on the front step when we got home. Two dozen. There's a card."

Emma opened the sealed envelope and pulled out the note. She read it silently. *Roses are red. Violets are blue. One more misstep and you'll be through.*

"Did His Royal Eminence send it?

Emma wondered the same thing. "It's not signed."

"Maybe Joshua?"

"No."

"Well, it looks like you have a secret admirer. I hope Joshua isn't the jealous type."

"I don't think so." In her spirit, Emma knew he wasn't, but her words lacked confidence.

"Tell me about him."

"There's not much to tell," Emma said. "Things just happened this morning . . . though I guess it's been brewing for a week or so."

"All I know is that he's a nice young man." Emma's mom paused. "He likes soccer, and he really likes you."

"I'm just getting to know him. But what's most important is I think we're at the same place spiritually and headed in the same direction."

"I can't begin to understand where you're at spiritually," her mom said as she folded one of Emma's favorite shirts—the long sleeve 'T' with an understated navy blue and white pattern. It was a gift from her grandma and filled her with joy each time she wore it.

"It's hard to explain," Emma said. "It started with me studying the Holy Text and then hearing the Sovereign's voice inside my head."

"Oh?" Her mom raised an eyebrow. Sometimes that meant disapproval, and other times it signaled confusion. "You've been studying the Holy Text?"

"Every night. I was afraid you wouldn't understand. You and Dad don't read it. No one I know does. Well, no one except Joshua and Sarah. And Gabe too. Oh, and Mrs. Butler. On top of that, you said normal people couldn't hear from the Sovereign. I didn't want you to think I was abnormal . . . or crazy . . . or something."

"I'm sorry you weren't comfortable telling us about it."

Emma shoved three pairs of jeans into a bag, on top of two pairs of shoes and a bunch of socks. That's when she noticed the twins hovering at the door.

Brayden spoke first. "Is Emma leaving?"

"I'm afraid so," their mom said.

"What if we don't want her to?" Hailey asked.

"Everyone moves out at some point," Mom

said. "We just thought it wouldn't be for a few more years until she went away to college."

Hailey's eyes popped open. "Is Joshua going to move in?"

Emma suppressed a laugh. "Nope." She stopped packing to give the sibs her full attention. "He's got his own family to live with. In fact, you may know his sister, Sarah. Sarah Hart."

"Sarah's his sister?" Hailey said. "She's in my English class and plays volleyball. She's kind of cool—and really tall."

Emma glanced at her brother to see if he might know Sarah too. He just stood there like a frozen statue, his face turning as red as a beet.

Hailey snickered and elbowed him. "Brayden's crushing on her."

He punched Hailey's shoulder and dashed away, with his giggling sister in pursuit.

With two bags packed, Emma proclaimed she had enough for now. "The only other things I need are my copy of the Holy Text and my journal."

Emma's mom retrieved the Scripture from its prominent stand on the shelf. Emma knelt next to her bed and slid her hand between the mattress and springs. She pulled out her cherished notebook.

Though she sensed her mom watching, Emma appreciated that she said nothing.

As an afterthought, Emma grabbed the two candles she used in her Scripture-studying ritual. She slid them, the Holy Text, and her journal into her backpack. She grabbed her laptop last. "I guess this will do for now."

"If you missed anything, we can bring it to the service next week." Her mom cleared her throat and blinked several times. She swallowed hard. "Or you can stop by after school. Anytime."

Emma turned away before she cried. "The limo should be here any minute. Let's head downstairs."

With her family gathered in the living room, Emma went to her dad first and gave him a tight hug. "Thank you. For everything. Love you."

"Joshua is a great guy," he whispered. "I approve." Then he gave her two quick pats on her back, signaling the end of their hug.

Emma went to the sibs next and embraced them at the same time. For maybe the first time ever, Brayden didn't squirm away. She kissed Hailey on the top of her head and gave her brother a quick peck too. He didn't complain.

Mom was last. Their hug was the longest. Neither spoke. Emma didn't know what to say and doubted she could talk without crying. Her mom probably felt the same way.

Her dad cleared his throat. "Limo's here."

As Joshua and the limo driver stowed her bags in the vehicle's trunk, Emma turned to face her family to give a final word. She swallowed hard. "I'm not sure if I'm leaving home or going home."

15

THE LIMO

Emma scanned the impressive vehicle from front to back, marveling over its length and its shimmering whiteness. It was oh-so white. "I've never ridden in a limo before."

"Me neither." Joshua rested his hand on the small of her back and guided her forward. The chauffeur opened the door for them.

Emma paused. "Are you Topher?"

"I am, My Lord," he said with a bow. "How did you know?"

"Someone told me the limo driver's name was Topher."

His voice rose in expectation. "Ashley?" His face brightened.

"I've already said too much." But before she

could stifle it, another spontaneous question spewed from her mouth. "Do you like her?"

"From afar," he answered. "But as long as we're both humble Temple servants, we're destined to be apart."

"Why?" Joshua moved closer to Emma and put his arm around her waist.

"His Royal Eminence prohibits marriage among the servants," Topher said. "Even if one of us were to leave our service to the Sovereign, the other would be too busy to date, let alone pursue a relationship or start a life together."

"I'm so sorry." Emma gave him a comforting pat on his upper arm. "It breaks my heart that you two can't be together."

Emma climbed into the limo but only moved part way in. Joshua squeezed in next to her. He tipped his palm up. That's all the encouragement she needed to place her hand in his. *I could live in this moment forever.*

As Topher eased the limo forward, he glanced at Emma in the rearview mirror. "Should I assume, My Lord, that we'll first drop off Mr. Hart at his residence?"

"Yes. Please."

"His Royal Eminence has briefed me, and I have the route mapped out."

Topher moved the car through the residential neighborhood, going well below the speed limit.

Emma considered their driver. "Topher, did you always want to be a chauffeur?"

"That's my father's gig. I was studying to be an accountant."

Emma perked up. "My mom is a CPA."

"I was in my last semester when Dad called one night. He had a run to make but felt dizzy. He asked me to fill in. I did. His dizzy spells worsened, and I covered for him more often. Eventually, I dropped out of school to work here full-time."

"How's he doing now?" Emma asked.

"Confined to bed."

"What do the doctors say?"

"He doesn't have insurance," Topher said. "We can't even afford an office visit."

"I thought all employers had to provide medical insurance." Emma cocked her head to the side.

"All but the Temple. They're the one exception."

"I didn't know that. That's terrible."

"We once had a clinic, though," Topher added.

"Well, we still do. It just hasn't been staffed for the last couple of years."

"My dad's a doctor. Maybe he can help."

"We can't afford it, My Lord. Besides, it wouldn't be proper."

Emma didn't see a problem. Surely her dad would want to help. She gazed out the window as she thought about the plight of Topher's dad and the injustice of the Temple not providing insurance.

As if sharing her concern, Joshua squeezed her hand.

She squeezed back.

Their leisurely drive through suburbia earned them much notice, with people turning to gawk and wave. Thrilled with the attention, Emma and Joshua waved back.

"I must point out, My Lord," Topher said, "that with tinted windows, no one can see you."

"Oh." Emma looked up at the sunroof.

"A smart solution," Topher said as it slid open.

Emma stood and poked her head through. Joshua joined her. They waved at everyone—both those who stared and those who waved first. Occasionally, someone would point, as if they recognized her.

"I wonder if this is what it's like to be a rock star?"

"You kind of are," Joshua said. "Embrace it."

An older car trailed behind them, matching their leisurely pace. When the driver didn't pass, Emma turned and waved at him. He didn't respond.

After a while, however, the allure of the attention and the novelty of waving faded. Besides, the brisk night air chilled them. Emma and Joshua slipped back inside the limo, and the sunroof slid shut, as if on cue.

Emma snuggled up to Joshua as he stretched his arm around her shoulder, pulling her tight. His closeness warmed her body—and her soul.

The last few days—without him and now with him—fluttered through her mind, like fast-forwarding through a video. Her thoughts paused on Joshua's release from jail. "When Captain Hernandez freed you, how many others were there?"

"Only three," Joshua answered. "Everyone else had already been sent to the retraining center."

"Mrs. Butler?"

"Already transferred."

Emma's expectation of a mass liberation

flagged. "Did Hernandez say anything about the other prisons across the country?"

"Most saw your request on television and complied. A few resisted, including the retraining center. I can text him for an update."

"He gave you his number? Was that in case you ever got in trouble again?"

Joshua laughed. "It was in case *you* ever got in trouble." He displayed the number, and Emma transferred it to her phone.

Their discussion ended when the limo coasted to a stop in front of Joshua's home. As Joshua exited the limo, Gabe stepped out of the house and walked with intention to the waiting car.

Topher held up a hand to stop him, but Emma offered correction. "It's okay. He's my friend. If he's looking for a ride, surely we can give him one. Besides, the two of us have some catching up to do."

"Very well, My Lord." Topher stepped aside, and Gabe joined Emma inside. She slid over to the far end of the seat, leaving a suitable gap between them.

16

ROY G BIV

"I'm cognizant that your day hasn't preceded according to your expectations," Gabe said, "but the particulars of the events that transpired are not yet clear."

"Going to school was much harder than I expected." Emma rubbed at her nose to distract herself—and Gabe—from the water that pooled in her eyes. "Some people hate me. They want me to leave."

Without asking for their destination, Topher eased the limo forward.

"Opposition to your standing as the first female High Priest is not unexpected," Gabe said. "Most people succumb to an irrational mentality to resist change."

"The good news is that I aced every assignment today. Perfect scores." Emma chose not to mention the threatening notes.

"You are an excellent student. Of that, I am most confident. Good grades, I deduce, are a common occurrence for you."

"But I didn't get marked down on a single thing all day. That's unusual, even for me."

"Receive it as the Sovereign's blessing as you navigate your bourgeoning position as High Priestess. Adjusting to your new reality will require both perseverance and patience."

"Oh, and I have a boyfriend!"

"You and young Joshua make a most impressive pair."

"I didn't say who."

"Yet my conclusion is not erroneous. There is no need for you to obfuscate."

Emma shifted in her seat. "Can we change the subject?"

"Present to me your query."

"What are the colors of the rainbow?" Emma pulled her notebook from her backpack and prepared to write. "In order."

"Roy G Biv. Do they not teach this generation anything of practical value in school?"

"Roy G Biv? Who's that?"

"It's a rainbow mnemonic. I'm quite sure that with careful consideration you can deduce its meaning."

"Let's see. R must be for red," Emma ventured, "and O for orange. Followed by yellow and then green. Blue, indigo, and violet last." She scribbled furiously in her notebook, making a column of the colors in rainbow order. "Roy G Biv."

She wrote *Gabe* next to yellow. After red, she added *Sarah*. Next to green she put *Chloe*. And *Joshua* after blue. Indigo was her parents' color, but what about the sibs? "Where does lilac fit?"

"Are you attempting to map each person's color manifestation in the spiritual realm with the rainbow in our physical reality? Spiritual colors exist without hierarchy or progression. Their mere existence matters most, followed by their intensity. Their shade aligns more with personality than anything else. Pay no attention to the hue."

"What about black?" Emma wrote *black* in big block letters at the bottom of her list. "Where's that fit in?"

"Black is the absence of any reflected color and of any spiritual presence," Gabe said.

"I see that many people have a dull black," Emma offered. "I think it's called flat black."

"Those poor souls are spiritually dead but not without hope."

"But one person's black has a shiny sheen," Emma said. "What does that mean?"

"It means to exercise extreme caution. An individual whose spirit shines black—a glossy black—in the supernatural realm is a person who has the evil one's spirit residing within. He is the most dangerous foe you will ever face."

Emma gasped. "Pompous Jack's spirit gleams with a slick black."

17

ANSWERED PRAYER

"Not to cause alarm, My Lord," Topher interrupted, "but the suspicious car that was following us earlier has returned. I've deviated from our chosen route twice, yet he continues to follow. Now a second vehicle has joined it. I'm suspicious of both. I want you to be aware of the situation."

"Thanks for letting me know. Don't worry. Go straight to the Temple Palace. The Sovereign will protect us. And please, please call me Emma."

"Yes . . . Emma," Topher said. "And so that I may plan, where should I drop off Mr. Gabe?"

"Thank you for inquiring, my good man," Gabe said. "My destination is the Temple. There I will invest the nighttime hours seeking an audience with the Sovereign, as I require additional clarity on the situation before us—"

A bump from behind interrupted Gabe. The limo lurched forward. The vehicle swerved, but Topher expertly tweaked the steering wheel to execute a quick correction and maintain control. A second jolt followed, more aggressive than the first. Emma's head jerked back as the limo blasted forward.

She turned and scowled at the car. Without thinking, she held up her hand toward it and thrust her palm forward. The car shuddered to an abrupt stop, as if it had hit a wall. The vehicle behind it rammed into it. The driver of the first car shook his fist as the limo drove on.

Once they were several blocks away, the cars moved forward, but they held back at a distance.

Emma extended her hands toward the heavens and looked up. "Oh, gracious Sovereign. Protect us and keep us safe from harm. Place a protective hedge around us and this vehicle. Also, please give Gabe the answers to his questions. We thank you for hearing us and for the answers you will provide."

"You are most wise for seeking the Sovereign for deliverance." Gabe's eyes shone with approval. "Now that you have requested what resides outside your control, your next course of action is to do what you can to mitigate the situation."

"There's nothing else I can do but pray."

"Carefully contemplate your response before reaching that determination."

Emma thought. A solution came to her. With a playful gleam in her eye, she pulled out her phone and sent a text to the captain.

"Human help is on the way too."

"Well done." That was the clearest, most succinct thing Gabe had ever said to her.

The two cars resumed their approach and zoomed toward the limo, but they could never get closer than about twenty feet, as if a force field held them at bay. Satisfied, Emma returned her attention to Gabe.

"Now, back to colors," Emma said. "I understand that color in a person's essence in the supernatural realm indicates the Sovereign at work in their life. And that black is the absence of it. What about their auras? Do those colors mean anything?"

"An aura reveals the presence of the Divine Spirit residing within the individual, figuratively shining out into the darkness. Save for two unique instances, color has no practical significance with auras either. The various hues carry no meaning, other than to demonstrate that each person is different, unique. The special cases are white and black."

Emma wrote *white* in block letters at the top of her list of colors. Since this was her aura, she added her name after it.

"Black is the absorption of all colors and the reflection of none," Gabe continued. "A person who gives off a black aura is evil, embodying the spirit of the devil. Correspondingly, white absorbs no colors and reflects all. From a philosophical perspective, white doesn't take and only gives. This signifies a person with a most intimate connection with the Sovereign."

An approaching siren interrupted them. A police cruiser with flashing lights pulled up behind the two cars. A second police vehicle soon joined the first. Topher pulled to the edge of the street and glided to a stop. Both suspicious cars zoomed past them, one speeding down the road at an alarming rate and the other squealing around the next corner to the right. In pursuit, the police cars sped by the limo.

"Thank you, Sovereign, for your protection," Emma said, "and for the captain sending help. Protect the officers and keep them safe as they do their jobs."

Topher guided the limo back to the street and moved forward at his usual leisurely pace.

"Addressing the topic of colors," Gabe said. "I earlier informed you that my estranged granddaughter has none. But today I spotted a pleasant hue emanating from her essence in the spiritual realm. This fills me with much unspeakable joy."

"Had you just not seen it before?" Emma asked. "Or was it new today?"

"Of this, I cannot be sure, for I usually only see her from afar."

As the limo made its way toward the Temple Palace, Emma and Gabe discussed passages from the Holy Text. Their exchange warmed Emma's soul and filled her with additional insight about how to reach up to the Sovereign and reach out to others.

In no time at all, the limo arrived at the palace. Awaiting them stood Pompous Jack, arms folded and the toe of his black designer shoe tapping on the sidewalk, with the sleek laces dancing at each rhythmic thump.

Another priest stood next to him.

Emma jumped out of the limo as soon as Topher brought it to a stop. She turned to face the frowning Pompous Jack.

"I understand you had a most arduous day," Pompous Jack said. "I trust that by now you understand the importance of staying at the Temple Palace and doing what I say."

"No, I don't. I'll only do what the Sovereign tells me to do. I don't care what you say or think."

Pompous Jack scowled. "Be that as it may, I'd like to introduce you to Junior. He'll be your new best friend from now on and go everywhere you go. If you disobey me, he will suffer the consequences you deserve. Think about that next time you go rogue."

18

MATCHMAKER

opher drove away to drop Gabe off at the Temple, and Pompous Jack stomped off, leaving Emma and Junior by themselves. To her delight, Junior had an aura. It was a vibrant orange. He stuck out his hand and looked straight at her. "Hi Emma, pleased to meet you."

She liked him right off. He accepted her as a person, not bowing, avoiding eye contact, or calling her *My Lord*. They would get along just fine.

Junior explained that Pompous Jack had instructed him to spend the night in the Temple Palace, just in case she needed him.

More likely to keep tabs on me.

Insisting it wasn't necessary, Emma urged him to return to his apartment on the grounds. She promised to go nowhere and wait for him in the morning. To seal the deal, she extended her smallest finger. "Pinky swear."

Junior laughed, linking his finger with hers. "Deal."

Emma watched him leave, went inside, and locked the door. She prepared for the next day, going to bed later than normal.

Morning arrived too soon, but Emma jumped out of bed, trying to convince her mind and her body to embrace the day. She showered quickly and headed to the palace dining room.

Jennifer was ready for her with two place settings at the table. "I hope I'm not being presumptuous."

"This is perfect. I like hanging out with you, and your food is a bonus." They sat down, and Emma extended her hand toward Jennifer. Jennifer grasped it, and Emma prayed. "Sovereign Lord, we thank you for this new day and ask for your blessings as we move through it. May we accomplish your will in all that we do. And protect us from evil and the evil one. Amen."

"Amen," Jennifer added in agreement.

As they dove into their food, Emma dove into some questions for Jennifer to better understand the situation with the Temple staff. "You said you're third generation. What was it like when your grandparents worked here?"

"They were some of the first people hired. Prior to that, the priests did all the work. But sixty or so years ago, the priests began hiring a few members of the laity to supplement their efforts."

"What do the priests do now?" Emma took a bite of toast and chased it with a gulp of orange juice.

"Aside from a weekly shift working in the ancient temple, not much. Some are serious gamers, others watch TV all day, and a few read. Mostly, they just expect us to wait on them." Jennifer cleaned up her yogurt and took a sip of tea.

"What about your parents?"

"My father oversees grounds and maintenance, and my mother manages food services. She's always short-staffed. That's why she plugged me in. By the time my parents arrived, the priests did little work, and the number of employees had grown. And now, the priests do no work, not even in a supervisory capacity. It seems we have about as many Temple servants as we do priests."

"I think there are two priests from each jurisdiction." Emma did a quick calculation. "That makes forty-eight total. Does that mean there's about fifty staff members too?"

"Let's see. Besides food services, there are maids, maintenance workers, and a grounds crew." Jennifer closed her eyes and moved her fingers as she counted. "A bookkeeper, communications director, cosmetologist, librarians, tech staff, laundry workers, and I'm sure I'm forgetting a few, but fifty sounds about right. Oh, there's also a security detail that reports directly to His Royal Eminence, but I don't think they're classified as Temple servants."

"And each one works seven days a week, receives no overtime, and is paid minimum wage for forty hours?" Emma popped a piece of melon in her mouth as she studied Jennifer's face for a reaction.

"Correct. His Royal Eminence demands much and keeps us hopping."

"How long has he been in charge?" Emma licked her lips and wiped them with her napkin.

"He had just arrived when my parents started. A lot has changed since then."

"It's not right."

"So true." Jennifer sipped the last of her tea. "But it's a sacrifice we're willing to make in service to the Sovereign."

"Did you always want to work here, like your parents and grandparents?"

"Quite the opposite," Jennifer said. "I earned my teaching certificate but couldn't find a job in the area and didn't want to move away from family. The Temple was hiring—they're always hiring—so I started working here. It was supposed to be temporary until I could get a proper job—I mean, a teaching job. But three years later, I'm still here."

Emma stopped herself before saying that's not right, something she'd been saying and thinking a lot for the working conditions at the Temple.

A man cleared his throat. Emma turned to see Junior standing in the doorway, a sly grin on his face. Ashley arrived just behind him.

"I guess this is my cue to leave," Emma said. She and Jennifer quickly cleared the table before she, Junior, and Ashley went out the front door where Topher sat in the limo, awaiting them.

"I'm not sure why you texted me to apply your makeup this morning," Ashley said. "It looks like you did a perfect job yourself. I like your fresh, minimalist approach."

"I may need a last-minute touchup when I get to school."

Topher opened the limo door for the three of

them. Ashley slid in first, but not before giving Topher a coy smile, which he returned.

"It looks like I have an entourage today." Emma slid in next and Junior, last.

As Topher drove toward school, Ashley whispered to Emma, "Are you playing matchmaker?"

Emma smiled. "I have no idea what you're talking about."

19

THE LOCKER

As the limo neared school, Emma turned to Ashley. "Please touch up my lip gloss. In case anyone asks, you can confirm I needed your help before school."

The car pulled to a stop in front of the building, attracting much attention. Curious students streamed to the gleaming limo, but when Emma got out, they dropped their gazes and recoiled.

"We don't want you here," called out a girl from within the crowd.

"Chicks shouldn't be High Priests," screamed an angry boy.

"You're messing up our school," another kid yelled. "Go back to your palace and stay there."

Emma turned to Topher. "Change of plans. I'll

walk home after school. Please pick me up there. And bring Ashley in case I need her." With that, she and Junior headed toward the building.

Murmuring discontent, the crowd parted to give them a wide passage to the main entrance of the school. When Emma walked inside, more students scurried away in hushed avoidance. "You'll have to sign in at the office," Emma said to Junior. "But I imagine they'll make you stay there all day."

"Perhaps they'll give me some work to do," he said. "It would be nice to be productive for a change."

As Junior signed in and explained the reason for his presence, Emma headed toward Principal Johnson's office. "I'm sorry for the commotion with the limo. It won't happen again."

"Speaking of commotion, My Lord, instead of disrupting the staff and stopping by my office to talk, just text me." He handed her a card with his number. "But it's for your use *only*. Understood . . . My Lord?"

"Yes, Principal Johnson."

"And His Royal Eminence phoned to explain the presence of your attendant, but as I told him, for the privacy of the other students, he'll need to stay in the office. I hope that is acceptable."

"If you give him something to do, I'm sure he'll be happy."

Emma hurried to her locker to pick up her English book so she could get to class, and everyone else could get to theirs. But she stopped short in front of her locker. Someone had drawn a noose on the door with a wide, black marker. She shuddered. Beneath it was "The End is Near" in bold letters.

With a smaller red marker, someone had crossed out *The* and written *Your* above it.

Sovereign, Emma whispered in her spirit, *protect me from this evil, and keep everyone else here safe too. Show me what to do.*

Let it go, came the ethereal voice from within that was also far away. *I've got your back.*

Shaking the tension from her shoulders, Emma pulled out her phone and snapped a picture of her desecrated locker. She texted it to Principal Johnson and to Captain Hernandez. She paused for a moment, blew all the air from her lungs, and gulped in a fresh supply before grabbing her book and heading off to English.

But she had trouble concentrating. The same for second hour history and third hour computer science. The tension she felt from the students on

Monday hadn't lessened. It was, in fact, worse. Much worse.

With five minutes left in computer science, she logged off and chucked everything into her backpack. She glanced up at Mrs. Thomas, who tipped her head toward the door with the slightest movement and made a subtle underhand gesture toward it, all without making eye contact.

Emma quietly exited, all the while feeling the glare of every other student. Chloe and Joshua stood waiting in the hall.

"Are you two skipping class?" Emma had to ask. "You'll get detention."

"Don't worry about us," Chloe said. "We're here to escort you to lunch."

"After what they did to your locker, we're not going to leave you alone for one more second." Joshua extended his hand, but she didn't take it. She wasn't sure how Chloe might react.

Clear out your locker, the Sovereign whispered to Emma.

"Let me get some stuff from my locker first," Emma said to Chloe and Joshua.

Someone, most likely the janitor, had scrubbed off most of the graffiti from her locker, but the outline was still there. Even though she had faith the Sovereign would protect her, Emma shuddered. She crammed all her personal items into her backpack, leaving only her textbooks behind. She'd grab them after sixth hour.

The trio got their lunches and headed outside. The rest of Emma's tribe—her disciples, as Gabe called them—soon arrived. They positioned themselves around her, as if giving her a ring of protection.

"There's a student petition going around school." William closed his eyes to recall the words. "It says, 'We, the undersigned, respectfully request that her Royal High Priestess cease attending Riverside High School, for her presence here is hampering our education.'"

"Are many people signing it?"

"Most everyone," William said. "I don't know what's wrong with them."

Emma took a sip of milk. "I don't blame them. It's clear I'm in the way. I asked Principal Johnson to give me a week for things to settle down, but I don't see that happening."

"Po-po," Lauren hissed to the group.

Captain Hernandez strode toward them. "I have an update. May I speak to the High Priestess privately?"

"It's okay for them to stay," Emma said. "I think this concerns them, at least indirectly."

Hernandez surveyed the group. "I fear you may be right. Each one of you may be at risk. Make sure I have your names before I leave."

He fixed his gaze on Emma. Replacing his hate-filled glare from last Saturday were soft eyes that emoted concern. "The security cams by your locker have been disabled. They've been out all week, so we can't identify the perpetrators. My team has, however, obtained a list of probable suspects, starting with those who yelled at you when you arrived this morning."

"Although I didn't like it," Emma said, "they have the freedom to voice their opinion. There's no crime in that."

"You are correct," the captain said, "but that does make them prime suspects in the threats against your person. I understand that last week you had an incident with one of them, Blaine Abernathy."

Chloe perked up. "That's right! He was harassing some new girl—a freshman, I think. But I don't know her name. Emma put a stop to it. She was amazing."

"Mr. Abernathy is our prime suspect among the

student body, but he lacks the mental acuity to execute these attacks with so much precision. Someone else is behind this, and we need to ascertain who."

"Aside from him being the school bully, I think he's harmless." At least Emma hoped so.

"I also investigated the young woman who was involved." Hernandez scrolled through his phone. "A Fahari Franklin."

"But she was the victim," Emma protested. "Why would you suspect her?"

"We considered the altercation to be staged specifically for your benefit, High Priestess—to draw you out and cause you to expose your . . . ah . . . shall we say your unorthodox beliefs." The captain made air quotes when he said *unorthodox*. "That would make her a suspect in the attacks against you."

"I'm sure she wasn't part of it." This knowledge came not from Emma's mind but from her spirit.

"I now agree with you." The captain nodded. "We've cleared her of any wrongdoing."

"Thank you for your hard work on this."

"As we continue the investigation, I remain concerned about your safety, High Priestess."

"The Sovereign has protected me so far, and I expect that to continue. And please call me Emma."

"I admire your confidence and your faith . . . Emma." The captain glanced away for a few seconds, but then he looked directly at her, the first time he had made sustained eye contact with her since the ordeal at the Temple. "You may want to consider distance-learning or homeschooling."

"You may be right. Thank you for the advice."

"My advice is for all of you." The captain swept his hand across the group as they huddled around Emma. "Given your relationship with the High Priestess, your safety may be at risk too."

20

PROTECTION

Captain Hernandez had spoken truth. Emma at last accepted the reality that she couldn't continue going to high school as if nothing had happened. She was no longer an ordinary student; she was the High Priestess. No one wanted her here, and she was no longer safe. She spent the last three hours of the school day watching the seconds tick by and didn't learn a thing. Her lone thought was to get out of there, all the while knowing she could never return.

At last, the bell rang. She intended to wait for the halls to clear before she left. But her disciples streamed into the room.

"We're going to make sure you get home safely," Isabella said.

"You might be better off keeping your distance." Emma sighed.

The normally quiet Kayla spoke next. "Not a chance." The others murmured their agreement.

Her disciples surrounded her. As a unit, they flowed down the hall to her locker. There, they stopped as one. The door was gone. Ripped off its hinges. Completely missing. A rope noose hung from the center hook. Red and black paint coated the inside of the compartment, dripping off her textbooks. In the wet paint along the back wall, someone had written with their finger, "You're next!"

Before Emma could react, Joshua took a picture and texted it to Captain Hernandez. "Maybe he can send someone to get a fingerprint."

"Let's get out of here." Chloe took a step away from the locker and led the procession down the hall. As they passed the office, Junior joined them.

"This is Junior. He's the priest assigned to me," Emma explained. "And Junior, this is everyone." Going left to right, she rattled off everyone's names, as Junior acknowledged each one.

Once outside, Emma tried to lead her posse like on every other day, but they refused to let her. Chloe took the lead instead, as the rest of them surrounded Emma. Joshua and Junior took up the rear.

"I appreciate this, but it's not necessary." Emma tried to speak with confidence. "The Sovereign will protect me."

"And we're going to help," came Joshua's response from behind.

"Thank you." Emma wasn't just being polite. She meant it. "The question for today—"

"We normally like our discussions," Lane said, "but I think we can skip it today."

Emma shook her head and smiled. "The question for today is 'How do you respond when others attack you?'"

A thoughtful conversation followed. Junior even took part, adding a few insights from the Holy Text. Her disciples' discussion encouraged her, and she hoped it benefited them just as much. By the time they reached Emma's house, all twelve remained. Each one had refused to leave her, even when they could have retreated to the safety of their own homes.

There sat the glistening white limo with Topher and Ashley in the front having an animated conversation. Topher spotted Emma. He jumped out but stopped short as he surveyed the group.

"Is there room for all of us?" Emma asked with a hopeful air.

"If you don't mind a tight squeeze." Topher opened the limo door, and the disciples piled in, bubbling with excitement.

With the back packed, only Junior remained outside. Ashley popped open the front door of the limo. "There's plenty of room up here." She slid as close as she could to the driver's seat. When Topher got in, she nestled up to him and tilted her head on his shoulder, letting out a contented sigh.

"Though this is not appropriate chauffeur etiquette," Topher said with a gleam, "I'm willing to make an exception, given the situation."

They dropped Chloe off first, as she lived the closest, and Joshua last, as he lived next to school. With all the disciples safely delivered to their homes, Ashley climbed in back with Emma and ran a quick comb through her hair. "Not that it needs my attention—at least not too much."

When the limo arrived at the Temple Palace, Pompous Jack awaited them at the top of the drive, arms crossed and lips pursed.

"Stay inside the limo," Emma whispered to Ashley. "Hopefully he won't see you, and you can avoid being sucked into my drama."

"You don't need to tell me twice." All the color blanched from Ashley's face. "Even in normal times, the way he looks at me just freaks me out."

For the first time, Emma waited for Topher to open the door for her so she could exit. As she emerged, she steeled herself to act as though she hadn't a care in the world. Thank goodness her theater training had prepared her for this role.

Pompous Jack glared at her. "I understand you've had quite a day," he sneered with disdain.

As Topher drove away in the limo, removing him and Ashley from the volatile situation, Emma glared back at Pompous Jack as Junior edged up to her. "What do you know about the kind of day I've had?"

"I can make it all go away in an instant." He raised his hand and snapped his fingers.

"Is that so?" Now it was Emma's turn to glare. "What's it going to cost me?"

"You silly teenager. All I'm asking for is a little quid pro quo."

"Quid, what?"

"To phrase it in your vernacular—something even you can understand—it means you scratch my back, and I'll scratch yours."

"Never. I don't trust you. And even if this back

scratching thing is a metaphor, the thought still grosses me out."

"Nevertheless, I hope that by now you understand how much you need my protection," Pompous Jack said.

"I don't need your protection. I have the Sovereign to protect me."

"Don't be naïve, my wee one. The protection I offer is real, not imaginary." Pompous Jack lowered his voice. "I've established a prestigious life for myself—one that others would kill for—and no sniveling little snot is going to get in my way."

Emma's soul flagged. Though she'd worked through one series of problems, a new one replaced it, one with life and death ramifications—and his name was Pompous Jack.

If you liked *Confronting the Chaos*, please leave a review online. Your review will help others discover this book and encourage them to read it too.

Thank you.

Chapter 1: Who's in Charge?

Emma had never liked Pompous Jack, and she certainly didn't trust him. But until now she had no reason to fear him. She locked eyes with the evil man. "That sounded like a threat."

"Oh, you so amuse me, little one. I never make threats, just promises." He stared down at her. The corners of his lips twitched up ever so slightly. "You can make this easy or you can make it hard."

"So can you!" Emma brought her hand to her hip and glared, just like she'd seen her mom do when she wanted to make a point.

"You're but an insignificant child. I won't

tolerate you telling a man of my stature what to do. Remember my standing as His Royal Eminence."

Junior stood next to Emma, but at a respectful half a step back. He served as the priest assigned to her, but this wasn't his fight. This contest was her versus Pompous Jack. She had no doubt.

What she wasn't sure about was if their confrontation was limited to the physical realm or if it would extend into the spiritual one too. According to Gabe, her trusted mentor, Pompous Jack's glossy black appearance in the spiritual realm confirmed he'd given himself over to the devil, whose presence filled his soul. This made him a most dangerous man, perhaps almost as dangerous as the devil himself.

"I'm also the High Priestess." Emma squared herself to him and narrowed her gaze. "According to the Holy Text, I'm in charge. You're not. So back down."

"Do you really think I care what that outdated tome says? Despite some antiquated book, I am, in fact, in charge. Once I prove you're a fraud, you'll be out of here so fast it will make your head spin."

Emma thrust her index finger at his gaunt face. "I can say the same about you." With the Sovereign on her side, she had nothing to fear. Still, concern taunted her for the first time since she had become the new High Priestess, a role she didn't want and wasn't ready for. Yet the Sovereign had picked her —a mere teenager—to lead the people.

With their eyes still locked, Pompous Jack spoke first, but without yielding in their contest of wills. "Are you going to stand here all night and stare at me?"

Normally, she'd be up for the challenge. Last time she bested him, but not tonight. Though she didn't want to blink first, the threats she'd endured at school all day left her emotionally drained. Persisting in a staring contest was the last thing she wanted to do. Exhaustion plagued her, and she looked away. Even more, she needed to recharge her soul. She would deal with him tomorrow.

"Go to your room!" He pointed a bony finger at the Temple Palace. "And if you know what's good for you, you'll stay out of my way."

"I'll only obey the Sovereign. I don't care what you say." Emma stomped off.

"Don't you dare walk away from me, you ungrateful brat."

Emma spun around and raised her chin. "Don't tell me what to do! I turn you over to the Sovereign for the punishment you deserve."

Pompous Jack's lanky frame sagged.

Emma left him standing in a daze at the palace entry. She marched toward the front door, with Junior striding to catch up. He reached the door first and opened it for her. She accepted his gesture with appreciation as he guided her to her quarters.

With head held high, she strode into the High Priest's residence in the palace, pulled the door shut, and clicked the lock. She exhaled slowly, slid to the floor, and cradled her head in her arms.

Oh, Sovereign, give me strength to stand against that evil man.

Continue reading *Dueling the Devil*, Book 3 of The Next High Priest Series.

ABOUT PETER DEHAAN

Peter DeHaan is an adult who dreams of being a teenager. When he's not contemplating grown-up thoughts, his mind retreats to the domain of invented worlds with his loyal and most real, yet still imaginary, friends. What grand adventures they have: righting wrongs, solving problems, and making their world a better place to live.

His first published adventures come to life in "The Next High Priest Series"—a faith-friendly speculative fiction adventure in a world just like ours . . . only different.

Next up is *The Curious Gift*, a YA contemporary novella with a hint of the supernatural.

Then comes "The Ice Creamed Series," a present-day quest for friendship and love, all the while trying to survive high school unscathed and ping-ponging between responsible impulses and irresponsible slipups.

Want more? Get a free short-story prequel about Emma along with news of upcoming books when you sign up to receive Peter's updates at PeterDeHaan.com/fiction.

FICTION BOOKS BY PETER DEHAAN

The Next High Priest

Seeking the Sovereign

Confronting the Chaos

Dueling the Devil

Reforming the Religion

Freeing the Prisoners

Fighting the Fanatics

Perfecting the Priesthood

Pursuing the Politicians

Restoring the Repentant

Get a free short-story prequel about Emma along with updates of upcoming books when you sign up for Peter's fiction newsletter at PeterDeHaan.com/fiction.